OPTIMISTIC OPHTHALMOLOGIST

A Satire

AROUET LE JEUNE

Optimistic Ophthalmologist

ISBN: Ebook: 979-8-9908813-1-0
Paper back: 979-8-9908813-4-1
Hardcover: 979-8-9908813-7-2

Book Cover Design and Interior Formatting by 100Covers.

To Lisa,

Whose love and support have been my anchor, this book is lovingly dedicated.

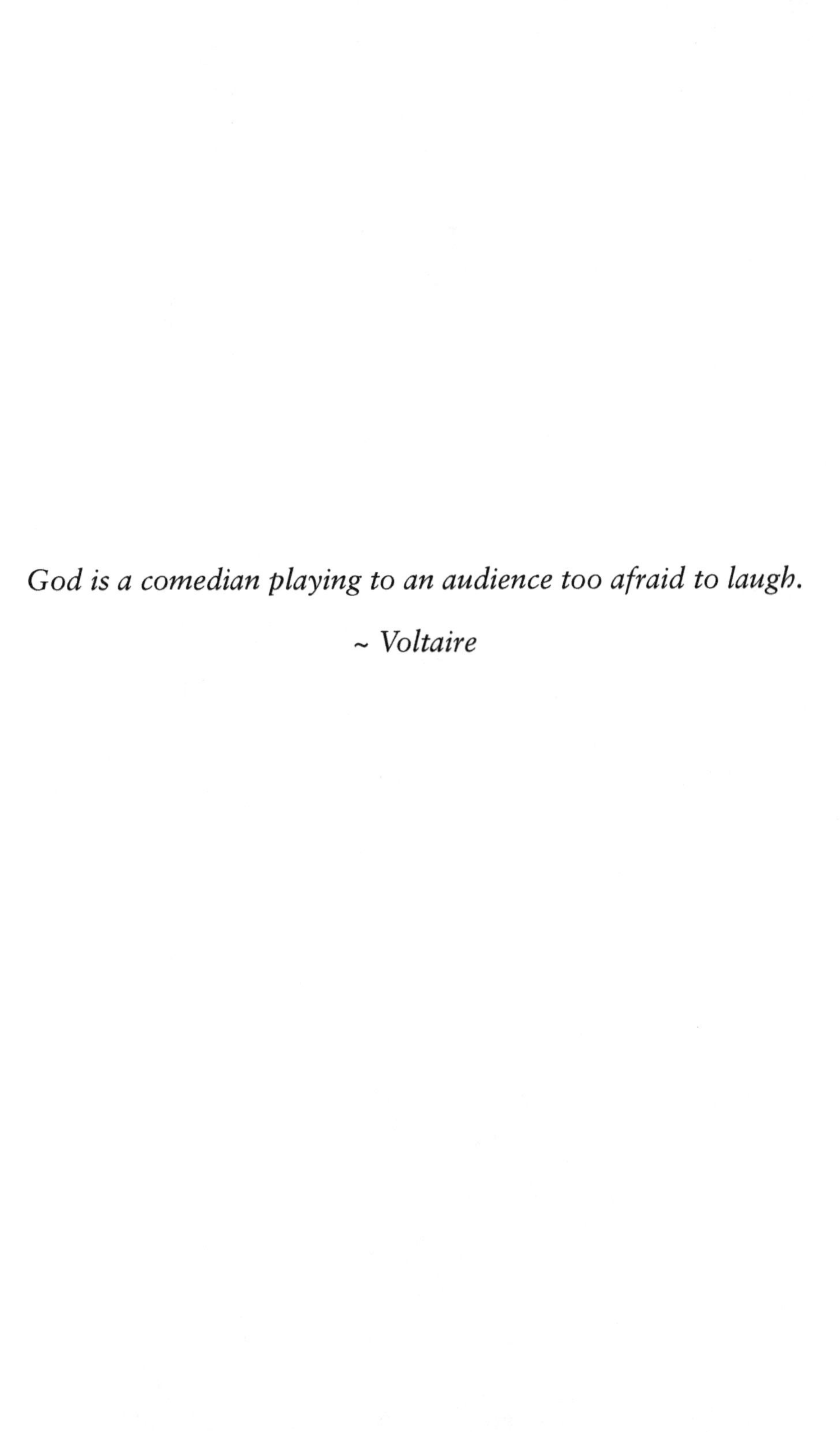

God is a comedian playing to an audience too afraid to laugh.

~ Voltaire

Contents

Chapter 1

When man was put into the Garden of Eden, he was put there with the idea that he should work the land; and this proves that man was not born to be idle.
~ Voltaire

Candide adjusted his graduation gown in front of the mirror, smoothing the fabric over his shoulders before donning the hood. He ran a hand through his mousy brown hair and crowned the graduation cap on his head, swinging the tassel from right to left with a flourish. A smile crept across his face—in one week, he would finish medical school. Beaming at his reflection, he exclaimed with a burst of joy, "Welcome to the club, Dr. Candide!"

His cell alarm went off. In a hurry, he removed the regalia down to his plain blue button-down shirt. It was time for class. *Let's finish strong,* he reminded himself.

He slung his backpack over one shoulder and headed out of his small studio apartment. As he walked across campus, he blended into the crowd of students rushing to their morning class-es. Candide had always been average—medium height, medium weight, mediocre grades, always a B minus, and an appearance as striking as a slice of white bread.

Standing at a perfectly ordinary height of five feet ten inches, his posture was neither slouched nor rigid. His weight was evenly distributed across a frame that neither flaunted the chiseled phy-sique of an athlete nor surrendered to the softness of a sedentary lifestyle. His features possessed an easy comfortable symmetry. His hazel eyes flickered between green and brown with the changing light. His eyebrows were neither too bushy nor overly groomed. His nose was straight without being sharp, and his lips held a natural curve that lent itself to a pleasant expression of mild contentment.

Candide slid into a seat in the back row of his pharmacology lecture. He took out a notebook and pen, ready to take meticulous notes as always. The professor, Dr. Pillzberg, droned on about medication side effects and interactions. Candide's hand cramped as he scribbled page after page of details.

In the row in front of him, two students whispered to each other.

"Did you hear about Pillzberg's research?" one asked.

The other shook his head.

"He's trying to prove vaccines cause autism. Can you believe that crap?"

Candide blinked. He had never encountered such blatant dis-respect at the World's Best Medical School before. Here, students were trained to be compliant, unquestioning physicians who ad-hered strictly to established medical doctrines. Unfazed, he simply continued taking notes, choosing not to engage in the controversy. His goal was straightforward: to keep his head down, get through school, and become a competent doctor. Nothing more, nothing less.

Candide walked out of the pharmacology lecture in a daze, his hand throbbing from all the frantic note taking. As he made his way across the quad, he overheard a group of students engaging in a heated debate about universal healthcare.

"It's a human right!" one girl insisted. "No one should be denied care."

Her friend scoffed, "And who's going to pay for that? It'll bankrupt the country."

Candide shuffled past without comment. He believed healthcare should be accessible to all, but voicing opinions could only lead to conflict. It was better to stay neutral. In the campus café, Candide grabbed an ice-cold bottle of water and ordered a turkey sandwich with white bread and mayo. As he waited in line, two young men in front of him argued about abortion.

"It's murder!" one said.

"It's a woman's choice!" the other shot back.

Candide pretended to study the café's menu and avoided eye contact. He didn't want to get sucked into another moral dilemma. His goal was to help people through medicine, not politics.

Finally, Candide escaped the crowded café and found an empty bench beneath a large, shady tree. As he unwrapped his sandwich, he took a deep breath and exhaled with relief. Gazing at the cloudless sky, he soaked in the warmth of the early New England summer. Surrounded by blooming flowers and a manicured lawn, he listened to the cheerful chirping of birds and watched the playful scurrying of squirrels. Here, he could eat in peace, far from the endless debates raging around him. Candide, a gentle soul, sought no quarrel with the world.

He took a bite of his sandwich, savoring the mayo in the momentary quiet. All around him, students buzzed with fervor for their causes: environmentalists, social justice warriors, and political activists. They devoted every free moment to protests, campaigns, and volunteering. Candide admired their dedication, but it wasn't for him. He was happy to keep his head down, focusing on his studies. As Candide finished his lunch, a group of students marched by, waving signs and chanting. He recognized them from the news on TV—they were boycotting a lecture by a controversial speaker from France.

No to Voltaire's words, we say nay;
His rhetoric, we will slay!

Candide gathered his things and headed in the opposite direction. He wouldn't join the boycott or defend the speaker; some battles weren't meant for him to fight. Back in his apartment, Candide opened his anatomy textbook. While other students partied on weekends, he was content studying. He had no interest in drinking, drugs, or casual relationships. While his classmates explored life's possibilities during their educational years, Candide remained single-minded in his pursuit of medicine.

In one aspect, Candide was unique among his peers. He'd remained a virgin, untouched by the hookup culture permeating the campus. Romance held little appeal for him. His fulfillment came from learning, from knowing he was on the path to helping others. Candide was an island unto himself, unmoved by the currents of passion and politics around him. All he wanted was to heal others.

Sitting at his desk, Candide reviewed his notes from a recent anatomy lecture, fascinated by the intricacies of the human body. He found it profoundly satisfying how each system worked in harmony to sustain life. He lingered on diagrams of the brain, awed by the command center that controlled thought, motion, and senses. He aspired to become a neurosurgeon, dreaming of the day he could operate on the organ that defines a person's identity.

A knock at the door interrupted his studies. It was the Chairman of the Board of the WBMS, Mr. Thunder-ten-tronckh, the world's richest man. "Do you have a minute, Candide?"

Candide welcomed him in. Mr. Thunder-ten-tronckh, a distinguished looking man in his late 70's had taken an interest in Candide. They'd had several conversations about Candide's goals and career plans.

Standing in the doorway, Mr. Thunder-ten-tronckh was a colossus of a man, towering over six and a half feet. His shoulders were broad as if chiseled from bedrock. His frame bore the solidity of an ancient redwood. His face was a map of lived experiences—lines etched deep by life's trials and triumphs. Under bushy, salt-and-pepper eyebrows resided sharp, piercing blue eyes that have retained their luminescence from youth, reflecting an intellect undimmed by time.

"I wanted to check on how your studies are going," Mr. Thunder-ten-tronckh said. "Are you still planning to go into neurosurgery after you graduate?"

"Yes sir, it's my dream." Yet Candide didn't have the standout resumé of other applicants. His test scores were mediocre, his extracurriculars, minimal. No one on the admissions committee could recall his name or ascertain the basis of his admission to the WBMS.

"Well, keep up the good work." Mr. Thunder-ten-tronckh squeezed his shoulder. "And if you need anything, let me know."

After he left, Candide considered the Chairman's special interest in him. Some speculated it was because Candide reminded Mr. Thunder-ten-tronckh of his own youth, a humble young man, a nobody. There were rumors that Candide was the Mr. T's grandson conceived out of wedlock, a product of Mr. T's oldest son, who was studying at the University of Westphalia, and a promiscuous local barmaid. But Candide didn't dwell on gossip. He simply appreciated having a mentor to guide him towards his goals.

Earlier in the year, Candide's acceptance into the World's Best Neurosurgery Residency through the National Resident Matching

Program baffled the software developers at NRMP. Although Candide was listed as accepted, his name was conspicuously absent from the applicant pool. After months of fruitless code revisions and countless program runs, the developers reluctantly admitted defeat, conceding it as an insurmountable glitch. Meanwhile, oblivious to the saga, Candide stayed focused on his studies, determined to make Mr. T proud one day.

Candide's focus was tested when he met Cunegonde. He was shadowing Dr. Storkheimer Wombwhisperer at the campus hospital, assisting in a delivery. The mother, a woman weighing 350 pounds, writhed and screamed as the monitors blared. Blood and amniotic fluid gushed everywhere. Candide's scrubs were soaked, and his head pounded from the chaos. During the final push, the mother let out a loud shriek, and one of her legs came loose from the stirrup, kicking Dr. Wombwhisperer in the forehead and knocking him out cold. The baby shot out like a human cannonball, flying across the delivery room. In a split second, Candide leapt and caught the baby in mid-flight with one hand, like an NFL wide receiver.

"Touchdown!" The room erupted in cheers and applause. A young nursing student stepped up to take the squirming newborn from his arms. It was Cunegonde, a petite nursing student with rosy cheeks. When she smiled at Candide, her ample bosom showed through her loose scrubs. Ashamed, he quickly averted his eyes back to the task at hand but couldn't shake the image of Cunegonde's beauty—her hair, a cascade of golden strands, absorbed the harsh hospital lighting and softened it into a halo around her angular face. Her irises were a clear azure, her nose delicate, with a slight upward tilt at the tip. Her lips were full and rosy pink.

"May I?" Cunegonde asked, as she took the wailing baby from Candide. Her voice had the cadence and melody of a bird song, gentle yet confident. Her figure was slender and graceful, moving with an effortless poise that bestowed her an ethereal presence.

Later that day, late at night, Candide went to the maternity ward to check on his most recent patient. As he entered the room, there was Cunegonde, cradling the newborn. When she saw Candide, her eyes lit up. She raised an eyebrow, tilting her head discreetly towards the door. After handing the baby back to the mother, Cunegonde stepped out of the room, her hips gently swaying.

Candide's heart quickened. Aroused, he knew he should resist, but desire overpowered reason. After a brief check on the tired mother, he followed Cunegonde to an empty on-call room, where they tumbled onto the lower bunk in a frenzy of passion. Time seemed to have stopped as they lost themselves in each other. Candide marveled at the thrill of intimacy for the first time.

But afterwards, guilt crept in. He had already jeopardized so much, and surveillance cameras were everywhere. Still, gazing at Cunegonde's sleeping form, he couldn't fully regret their encounter. For that moment, he had experienced ecstasy.

The next morning, Candide was summoned to Dean Pangloss's office. His stomach churned with dread as he knocked on the door.

"Come in," boomed the Dean's voice.

After taking a hard gulp, Candide entered. Dean Pangloss, a tall man in his 60's with a head of silver hair, sat behind a massive oak desk, hands clasped in front of him, his expression grave.

Dean Pangloss possessed a formidable presence, yet there was an alluring eccentricity to him—an air of authority mingled with an enigmatic charm. He dressed impeccably, in a three-piece suit of the finest tweed, molded to his lanky frame. His vest clung to his torso, the buttons straining ever so slightly against a dignified paunch that bespoke of a life well-lived and meals well-digested.

"Have a seat, Candide," he said, gesturing to a chair facing the desk.

Candide sat down gingerly, pulse racing.

The Dean cleared his throat. "It seems there was an . . . incident yesterday involving you and a certain nursing student."

He turned his computer monitor to face Candide. There on the screen was footage from the on-call room. Candide stared barely blinking, cheeks burning.

"This is a clear violation of our code of conduct," continued the Dean in a slow steady cadence as if he were a courtroom judge. "Relations between students while on duty cannot be tolerated. You have jeopardized the sanctity of the WBMS and defiled a young woman."

Candide hung his head. "I'm sorry, sir. It won't happen again."

The Dean sighed. "Unfortunately, given the competitive nature of our neurosurgery program, the World's *Best* . . . (and he hesitated for emphasis on *Best*) . . . Neurosurgery Residency, I'm afraid this lapse in judgement has cost you your residency position."

Candide's head shot up in alarm. "But sir, neurosurgery is my dream!" he pleaded. "Please give me another chance."

The Dean held up a hand. "The decision has been made. We only accept candidates with the purest of heart and the utmost professionalism. Your . . . urges . . . render you unfit."

Candide blinked back tears, as his vision of the future came crashing down around him. The Dean droned on about rules and conduct, as well as ethics and responsibility, but he sat numb; all he could think of was Cunegonde. He knew he should be paying attention, but his mind kept drifting back to her. *Where is she now? Has she been expelled?*

Finally, the Dean's tone softened. "Now Candide, don't despair. I know this seems bleak, but truly this is for the best. I've found you an ophthalmology residency instead. A smaller organ like the eye should be easier for you to handle. It would require less of you emotionally, something more suited to your . . . recent lack of self-control."

With hesitation, Candide looked up at Pangloss. Ophthalmology had never interested him, but beggars couldn't be choosers. "Th-thank you, sir," he stammered. "I appreciate you finding me an alternative."

The Dean gave him a benevolent smile. "Of course, my boy. All is for the best, in the best of all possible worlds. You'll see."

Candide nodded, though he didn't quite believe it yet. There was still one question haunting him. "Sir?" he ventured. "What happened to Cunegonde?"

The smile faded from the Dean's face. "Ah, yes. The young lady has been dismissed from the nursing program and left the dormitories last night." His tone made it clear that the subject was closed.

Candide felt his heart crack. His foolishness had ruined Cunegonde's future as well. They'd never get another chance to be together now.

"I understand," he said quietly. "Thank you for your time, sir." He left the office, stunned, the Dean's reassurances ringing hollow in his ears. Cunegonde was gone, his career destroyed—*how could this be the best of all possible worlds?*

A few days later, Candide boarded a plane with a heavy heart, heading south to begin his ophthalmology residency at the World's Best Eye Institute.

He took his window seat and stared blankly out at the tarmac, still struggling to process everything that had happened. He had worked hard for years to get into the top neurosurgery program, only to have it ripped away in an instant. And Cunegonde—his dear, sweet Cunegonde—was *gone*. He had no idea where she was or if he would ever see her again.

As the plane accelerated down the runway, Candide pressed his forehead against the window, willing himself not to cry. The past few days had been a whirlwind of shame and despair. He kept replaying his tryst with Cunegonde in his mind—her coy smile, the feel of her skin, their hurried fumbling in the dark. It had been the most glorious experience of his life. But now, he regretted letting passion override reason. If only they had been more careful, more discreet.

The plane leveled and the seatbelt sign dinged off. Candide sighed deeply. What was done was done. There was no changing it now. He had to accept this new path, as foreign and punishing as it felt. As Dean Pangloss said, it was all for the best. Candide had always been perfectly average, unremarkable in every aspect. Maybe ophthalmology was where he would make his mark.

Still, as the plane flew further away from everything and everyone he knew, Candide couldn't shake the feeling that a piece of his heart had been left behind. He gazed out at the clouds, tears filling his eyes. His future looked so uncertain now.

Chapter 2

*Men will always be mad, and those who think they
can cure them are the maddest of all. ~ Voltaire*

Candide stepped off the plane and into the sweltering heat of
Miami. The oppressive humidity wrapped around him like a wet
blanket, a sharp departure from the crisp, early summer morning
air he had left in Boston three hours earlier. Squinting against the
glaring sunlight, he made his way across the tarmac toward the
main terminal.

Inside, the baggage claim was bustling with activity. Travelers
crowded around the circling conveyor belts, jostling for position as
they waited for their luggage. Stood off to the side, Candide wiped
beads of sweat from his brow, relieved he had packed light—a
small roller bag and a backpack. From the corner of his eye, he
noticed two buff airport porters approaching him, one tall and the
other short, both clad in striking red uniforms.

"Dear sir, welcome to Miami. Let me help you with those bags," said the short porter with a broad smile. Before Candide could respond, the man had already grabbed his roller bag and heaved it on a roller cart.

"Oh, um, thank you," Candide replied.

The tall porter reached for Candide's backpack. "We'll take good care of your luggage, sir. Where are you heading?"

"The World's Best Eye Institute. I'm going to start my residency tomorrow," Candide eagerly replied.

"That's a fine dandy place. My parents had their cataracts done there. We'll bring these right out to you by the taxi stand, OK Doc?"

Without hesitation Candide handed over his backpack. "Okay then. I'll be right outside. Thank you for your help."

"Not a problem at all, sir," the first porter said. "You have a great day now."

Candide gave them a nod and turned towards the exit. As he stepped outside into the harsh sunlight, the porters were nowhere to be found. After waiting for twenty minutes, the unsettling truth dawned on him: he had been duped. Those "porters" had seemed a little too helpful. Now his luggage and backpack were gone.

"You've got to be kidding me," Candide muttered under his breath. This was not the fresh start he had envisioned. After an hour at the taxi stand with no luck, frustrated and weary, he had no choice but to proceed on foot. The World's Best Eye Institute was six miles away. With a resigned sigh, he began his lengthy trek toward the WBEI, relying on the GPS on his cell phone to guide him.

As Candide trudged along the sidewalk, sweat trickled down his back under the oppressive humidity. After covering about a mile, his mouth turned parched and his stomach growled, reminding him he hadn't had anything to eat or drink since leaving Boston.

Wiping his brow, he scanned his surroundings desperately for any sign of a store or café.

"Excuse me sir, can you help us?"

Candide turned toward the voice and saw a man and woman standing there, looking lost. They appeared to be tourists, both sporting sunglasses. The man in a Tommy Bahama shirt paired with long white pants, while the woman wore a form-fitting floral dress cut at mid-thigh.

"We are trying to find the art museum," the woman said in a heavy Eastern European accent. "Do you know which way is it?"

Candide hesitated. He was new to Miami, but he felt sorry for this couple. They seemed so helpless.

"I'm not totally sure . . . " he began.

As he spoke, the man sidled up close to him and put a hand on his shoulder. "Please, can you just show us on our map?" he asked, pulling out a city map and unfolding it before Candide. As Candide leaned in to examine the map, he pulled out his cell phone to use the GPS to locate the museum.

"I think it's this way . . . " he muttered as his thumbs tapped the phone. While his eyes were fixed on the screen, he didn't notice the woman's hands dipping into his pockets. In a flash, she had snatched his wallet and the last few dollars he had on him.

"I think it's right over here . . . " he handed his cell phone to the man and pointed to the screen.

"I see it now! Thank you!" the man nodded.

"Yes, thank you, sir!" the woman added.

Before Candide even grasped what had happened, the couple hurried off down the street and disappeared into the crowds.

Candide's hand went to his pocket where his wallet had been moments before. He had also forgotten to ask for his cell phone back.

"You've got to be kidding me," he muttered again. Pickpocketed by two gypsies pretending to be tourists. *Could this day get any worse?* Now completely bereft of money and possessions, he noticed the city map the pickpocket had dropped. Picking it up, Candide opened it. At least he could navigate with that. With no other options, he continued his long walk to the Eye Institute.

By late afternoon, the temperature had soared to 100 degrees. The air grew heavier and more humid, and the sun glared down like the eye of a cyclops. After walking four miles from the airport, Candide was thirsty, sunburnt, drenched in sweat, and utterly exhausted. He stripped down to his T-shirt and longed for a pair of shorts. Having spent his entire life in the cool Northeastern climate, he was unprepared for the sweltering tropical heat of Miami.

Moments later, Candide was elated to spot a big box supermarket ahead with its sign lit up like a beacon. With the little energy he had left, he pushed toward that urban oasis. When he entered the large, modern grocery store, he was close to passing out from heatstroke, but the blast of cool air quickly revived him. As he walked towards the refrigerated section to grab an ice-cold bottle of water, a flash mob of hundreds burst through the front entrance. They proceeded to ransack the supermarket, overwhelming the hapless security guards, beating up the customers and robbing them blind. Caught in the chaos, Candide managed to crawl into a meat locker for safety. He huddled there in the cold and dark, listening to the mayhem outside. After what seemed like an eternity, the flash mob left, and police sirens wailed like banshees in the distance.

Candide stayed hidden, unsure if it was safe to come out. His empty stomach rumbled, and his parched throat ached for water, yet he remained huddled in the cold meat locker for over an hour. His body was frozen, his limbs stiff and numb, but he didn't dare leave his hiding spot until he was sure the danger had passed.

Finally working up the courage, Candide cautiously opened the locker door and peered outside. The supermarket was eerily quiet, with ransacked shelves, smashed displays, overturned shopping carts, and aisles littered with debris. Bloodied bodies of customers and store crew were scattered about, stark reminders of the earlier pandemonium. Creeping toward the front of the store, Candide saw flashing police lights through the glass doors. As he was about to reach the entrance, two officers burst in, guns drawn. Startled, Candide instinctively threw his hands up.

"Don't move!" one officer yelled, keeping his pistol aimed right between Candide's eyes.

"I didn't do anything!" Candide froze, pulse racing as he stared down the barrel.

"Shut up!" the second officer barked. He grabbed Candide by the neck and slammed him against a nearby shelf.

Candide winced as jars of tomato sauce shattered around him, covering him in a pasty red. "Please, I was just hiding in there during the riot!" Terrified, he pleaded, pointing to the open meat locker door.

The first officer scoffed, "Yeah right, you were probably part of that mob!"

Before Candide could protest further, the first officer's fist plunged into his solar plexus. Candide grunted, doubled over, gasping for air. The officer followed with an upper cut to Candide's chin. His head snapped back like a ragdoll. As he struggled to stand, the second officer kneecapped him with a baton and kicked his legs out from under him. Candide collapsed to the floor, shards of broken glass cutting into his skin.

The two officers continued the beating, fists and batons landing in sickening thuds, oblivious to his cries for help. Candide's vision started to blur, all consciousness fading.

"That's enough!"

The officers abruptly halted their assault. Bleary-eyed, Candide looked up to see a police sergeant standing over him, frowning.

"You idiots, this man is an eye doctor. Look at his T-shirt. He is from the World's Best Eye Institute," the sergeant said.

The first officer glanced down at Candide's T-shirt emblazoned with the WBEI's logo and scowled. He pulled Candide up by his hair and delivered one last hard kick to Candide's behind.

"Get out of here!" the sergeant ordered.

Battered and bruised, Candide stumbled out of the ransacked supermarket and into the dark night, the officers' cruelty haunting his every step. He couldn't believe what had happened to him. All he wanted was to quench his thirst and to cool off from the oppressive heat. He had never committed any crime, not even a moving violation. But tonight, he was violated.

Limping down the dimly lit street, each step sending shock-waves of pain through his bruised body, Candide had a pounding headache and ringing in his ears. He could barely move his jaws, his tongue was cut, and some of his teeth were loose. He winced, as he gingerly touched his swollen-shut eye and split lip. Blood trickled down his forehead. His ribs and back screamed with every labored breath. He needed medical attention for his injured eye, but the World's Best Eye Institute was still miles away. He had lost his map, and his foggy mind struggled to remember the way to the WBEI.

Exhausted and despairing, Candide slumped against a graf-fitied wall and slid to the ground. He had endured so much mis-fortune since arriving in this unfamiliar city. He first whimpered, then sobbed as he recalled the night with Cunegonde. He missed her beautiful angular face, her expectant blue eyes, her rosy pink lips, and her warm supple skin. He wished he were still a student at the WBMS, enjoying a turkey sandwich with mayo under the tall shady tree.

A chorus in the distance interrupted his reverie. He glanced around with one eye open. A group of men, dressed in black frocks from head to toe and singing in unison, was marching toward him. Candide cried out, begging them for help. The group halted, their eyes fixed on his disheveled figure. The leader knelt to inspect the mangled mass of humanity before them.

"Son, do you believe in the Holy Trinity?" he asked with utmost solemnity.

Candide, who had never read the Bible, racked his befuddled brain. Desperate, he blurted out, "Yes, I believe in the Holy Trinity. Please save me!"

"Sorry son, wrong answer. May God have mercy on you." After leaving a pamphlet by his side, they left Candide where they found him and continued their march, singing praises to the All Mighty in unison.

We gather here, a quirky mix, in search of truth so wide,
From cosmic dust to sacred texts, with coffee by our side.
With open minds, we welcome all, the serious and the jest,
Unitarian Universalists, in questioning we're blessed.

Hallelujah, Amen, pass the bean dip, please,
In our spiritual buffet, we sample as we please.
No dogma can confine us, in diversity we're dressed,
Unitarian Universalists, in loving jest we jest.

Candide took a glimpse of the front of the pamphlet which read, "Welcome to the World's Best Unitary Church. We are one under God." As he contemplated giving up, a homeless man shuffling by noticed the logo on Candide's T-shirt. "You headed to the eye place, son?" he asked in a gravelly voice.

Candide nodded weakly.

"It ain't too far now. C'mon, I'll help you get there," the old man said, offering a strong gnarled hand.

Candide wavered, then took it, too tired to refuse assistance. Leaning heavily on the stranger's shoulder, he persevered down the street. The man patiently supported him, sharing stories to distract Candide from the pain. Along the way, Candide saw the sides of the street, lined with rows of tattered tents and makeshift shacks. In them were the homeless, the drug addicts, the abandoned, the deranged, gaunt and emaciated, all enveloped in a thick stench of uncollected garbage and human waste. The denizens of the makeshift camp stared vacantly at the odd pair as they hobbled past.

Finally, the WBEI's glowing sign came into view. The old man got Candide to the door and waved farewell. Candide mouthed *thanks,* then stumbled inside, collapsing in relief. Though misfortune had battered him, kindness had seen him through. Now he could finally get treatment for his injured eye, in time to start his residency training. Pangloss was right. The long journey had been worth it after all.

Chapter 3

All is for the best, in the best of all possible worlds.
~ Pangloss

Candide awoke to the steady beeping of monitors and the sting of antiseptic in his nose. He tried to open his eyes but only one complied, the other crusted shut with dried blood and pus. As his vision adjusted to the bright fluorescent lights, he found himself in a hospital room, his battered body encased in casts and wrapped in bandages.

An IV bag dripped clear fluid into the tube in his arm, while a catheter drained his yellow urine into a bag below his bed. He could barely move; his jaw was wired shut, and his back was immobilized. He experienced no pain, thanks to the narcotics being pumped through his veins—a small mercy in the grand cacophony of misfortune that had befallen him.

A bearded man sat at his bedside reading a book. Candide recognized him as the shabby homeless man who had helped him. *What is he doing here?*

The man looked up and smiled. "Welcome back! We were starting to worry you might never wake up." His voice was kind, familiar.

The disheveled man by his bedside was a figure who seemed carved from the stones of hardship and weathered by time. His beard, an unkempt cascade of salt-and-pepper hair, flowed like wild vines over a battered denim jacket. The lines on his face were deep as canyons. His eyes sparkled with mirth that spoke of divine joy, with a hint of resignation and sadness. Framed by thick eyebrows, his gaze held Candide's with both gravity and warmth.

Candide tried to speak but could only groan through his wired jaw.

"No need to talk," the man said. "I'm Jake, Jake Anabaptiste, we met the night you were attacked. I'm a doctor here at the World's Best Eye Institute. I've been checking in on you."

Candide's one good eye widened in surprise. *This scruffy homeless man is a doctor?*

Jake chuckled, seeming to read Candide's mind. "I know, I don't look the part. That's by design. I work with the homeless population. I dress down like this to gain their trust. I was on my way back from the shelter when I found you a few nights ago."

Candide blinked gratefully. So, this man had saved his life. He owed Jake everything. Without him, Candide would have been dead, his plan of becoming an ophthalmologist and reuniting with Cunegonde—destroyed.

Jake patted Candide's blanketed foot. "Kid, you've got a long recovery ahead but you're in good hands now. I'll be here to help, my friend."

Tears stung Candide's good eye. Even in his darkest hour, providence had sent this guardian angel to watch over him. With Jake by his side, hope seemed possible once more.

Jake's kindness and humility deeply impressed Candide during his long recovery. Though Jake was a renowned eye surgeon who could work anywhere, he chose to devote himself to the poor and homeless. Jake was also the head of the WBEI. Under Jake, the WBEI treated every patient regardless of ability to pay.

When Candide was finally able to leave his hospital bed, Jake began taking him on weekend trips to check on the city's homeless population. One chilly Saturday morning they came upon a pathetic soul—an elderly man lying face down, unconscious inside a makeshift cardboard shack. As Candide turned the man over, he recoiled at the sight. The old man's face and entire body were covered in oozing pustules, his right eye porcelain white. Jake examined the man and concluded he had a severe case of syphilis.

"Poor soul," Jake murmured. "He's completely deaf in one ear too. We need to get him help." Candide nodded, suppressing his disgust at the man's festering sores. But after all he had endured, how could he judge another's suffering? The two of them gently loaded the elderly man into the van. As they drove toward the hospital, Candide felt grateful for the providence that had saved his life by bringing Jake to his aid. Now, he had the chance to repay that mercy by helping this destitute stranger in return.

The elderly man stirred as they carried him into the emergency room. His one seeing eye blinked open and focused on Candide.

"Candide!" he croaked, sitting up with a sudden burst of energy to embrace him.

Candide flinched, the man's oozing sores smearing Candide's pristine white coat.

"Don't you recognize me?" the elderly man pleaded. "It's me, Dr. Pangloss!"

Candide hesitated, staring at the pitiful creature before him. Could this be the esteemed Dean of the World's Best Medical School? The man who had taught him everything he knew about how the world works in general and medicine in particular?

Pangloss gripped Candide's arm, desperation in his rheumy eyes. "My dear Candide, what's happened to me? What's happened to you?"

Pity swelled in Candide's chest. "Dr. Pangloss," he said gently. "You are at the WBEI being treated for tertiary neurosyphilis. I'm so sorry to see you in this state. Please tell me, what misfortunes brought you so low? And do you have any word of Cunegonde?"

Dr. Pangloss shook his head with a look of sorrow. "So much has befallen us, my boy. Where to begin . . ." Candide's dismay grew as his mentor recounted betrayal, disease, and loss. Yet the uplifting tone of optimism in Pangloss's voice, along with the belief that all was for the best in this world, resonated with Candide. Providence had brought them together again for a reason.

"After you left the WBMS, things took a dark turn. Shortly after your departure, I too had an illicit tryst with a lovely young lady, Paquette, the voluptuous personal secretary to Mr. Thunder-ten-tronckh, an ecstasy I would never forget." Pangloss paused, his eyes gone soft with rapture before he continued. "Unfortunately, the entire episode was captured on surveillance video. Mr. T summarily dismissed me the following morning. Now I find that she gave me this syphilis that's ravaged my body as a punishment for my indiscretion." He paused again, seeing the shock on Candide's face.

"Yes, I have fallen far from the virtuous man you once knew. But that's not the worst of it . . ." Pangloss averted his eyes, voice cracking. "Cunegonde is dead. There were complications with her pregnancy, and she hemorrhaged during a botched abortion. I'm so sorry, my boy."

With this Candide reeled, grief crashing over him in waves. His darling Cunegonde, gone forever. The future they might have shared—wiped out in an instant. He turned on Pangloss in anguish. "How can you still cling to your optimism in the face of such senseless tragedy? What possible good could come of this?"

Pangloss placed a comforting hand on Candide's shoulder. "My boy, you must have faith. Our sufferings are but a small part of life's grand design, far greater than we can comprehend. Take heart, for you and I have found each other again. Providence has more goodness in store, if we have the courage and the patience to see it."

Candide searched his mentor's face through tear-filled eyes. Pangloss was right. If their reunion was any indication, there might yet be light on the horizon.

Pangloss went on, his voice growing stronger. "Consider how my affliction brought us the cure of penicillin, saving countless lives. And the tragic death of dear Cunegonde will spur doctors to prevent such accidents, sparing other women her fate. Her memory will drive you to heal and comfort the afflicted, will it not?"

Candide nodded. "I see the truth in your words. Her loss pains me deeply, but I will channel that grief into caring for the suffering, as you taught me."

Pangloss smiled. "That's the spirit, my boy." He gestured for Candide to help him to his feet. "Come, give me a lift and take me to the clinic. With some rest and medicine, I'll be myself again in no time."

At the hospital, Pangloss submitted to tests and treatments. They drained his sores, cultured his blood, and tapped his spine. The diagnosis was clear: advanced tertiary neurosyphilis. They removed his blind eye, fitting a prosthetic in its place. With antibiotics and proper care, his mind and body began to heal.

Throughout his recovery, Candide tended to his mentor daily. The old man grew stronger, his wisdom intact. Though still mourning Cunegonde, Candide's heart swelled with newfound purpose. With all his energy, he poured himself into his residency. He read voraciously, attended every round, kept up with the latest diagnostic methods and treatment modalities. He spent countless hours in the wet lab perfecting his surgical skills. He watched every YouTube video on eye surgery to learn the best techniques. He vowed to devote his service to mankind as a tribute to Cunegonde. With Pangloss as his guiding light once more, he would embrace the future's possibilities.

A few months later, Pangloss had fully recuperated, regaining his mental faculties and physical stamina. Jake, impressed by Pangloss's resilience and wisdom, hired him as a professor at the WBEI. Upon hearing the news, Candide was elated to have his mentor nearby to guide him through his ophthalmology residency, just as he had guided Candide through his years at the WBMS. Pangloss attended Candide's rounds, offering encouragement and advice. His knowledge of medicine was encyclopedic, and his experience extensive. His oratory skills were as sharp as ever. Holding doctoral degrees in medicine, philosophy, law, and divinity, Pangloss exuded a contagious optimism. He soon became the most favored faculty member at the WBEI, with professors and residents alike seeking his counsel on all matters.

Sometime later, Jake, Pangloss and Candide were on a flight to Haiti on a month-long medical mission to perform charity eye surgeries for the local poor. En route, Jake and Pangloss debated on the nature of evil and suffering.

"I don't accept that misfortunes are somehow part of a greater plan," Jake argued. "Too much agony springs from selfishness and greed. God may have given us the tools to slaughter each other, but we wield them by choice."

Pangloss shook his head. "You underestimate the intricate connections underpinning our reality. Cause and effect ripple forward and back through time in ways we can scarcely comprehend."

Candide listened intently, weighing their perspectives. Since losing Cunegonde, he found truth in both views. But he took comfort in knowing that whatever life brought, he had wise counsel to help him make the best of it. As the debate grew heated, Candide gazed out the window. Dark clouds were gathering on the horizon, lightning flickering within their billowing forms. As they descended towards Port-Au-Prince, the turbulence increased.

Pangloss and Jake fell silent, noticing Candide's distraction. They joined him, peering out at the encroaching storm. The clouds now shrouded the coastline as rain pelted and wind buffeted the plane.

A frantic voice came through the intercom: "Ladies and gentlemen, this is your captain speaking. Please return to your seats and buckle your seatbelts . . ." Before the captain could finish, a lightning bolt struck the plane, causing the power to go out. Seconds later, the left engine caught fire. The plane listed briefly in midair, like a bird shot in flight, before spiraling slowly for a moment and then plunging straight toward the dark, turbulent sea.

Chapter 4

Life is a shipwreck, but we must not forget to sing in the lifeboats. ~ Voltaire

Candide gasped for air as the water rushed into the cabin. The tail of the plane, barely above water, groaned and creaked, threatening to break apart at any moment. He scanned the dim interior, spotting Pangloss and Jake clutching onto seats to avoid being swept away by the swirling torrent.

A flight attendant emerged from the rear of the plane, terror in her eyes. "We need to get out of here now!" she yelled over the roar of the water.

"There's a life raft under the rear seats," Jake shouted. "Help me launch it!" Together, they strained against the weight of the raft as the water rose to their chests. With a final push, it plopped into the frothing sea—and promptly sank.

The flight attendant's arms flailed in the water, her face pale as a ghost. "Gone," she sputtered, coughing up saltwater. "It's gone!"

Candide, shivering, his muscles numb and tight, squared his jaw against the despair threatening to overwhelm them all. "We still have the emergency exit," he said, pointing toward the painted sign above their heads. "We can inflate our life vests and float to the surface."

Pangloss, ever the philosopher even in moments of life-threatening crisis, nodded with a grim determination. "Indeed, Candide," he replied, hoisting himself up the inclined aisle as the water sloshed violently around them. "The possibility of perishing in the attempt does not preclude us from making it."

Jake reached over and tore at the handle of the emergency exit, pulling with all his might against the pressure of the water outside. With a loud pop and a rush of air, the door gave way, and a torrent of water cascaded in. As they surfaced gasping for air, the raindrops pummeled their faces like a barrage of fine needles and the violent sea churned, threatening to pull them under.

A giant rubber ducky float popped to the surface near them, having escaped from the plane's cargo hold. Pangloss clambered in first, offering a hand to pull Candide aboard. Jake gripped the flight attendant's arm, dragging her onto the bobbing raft. They huddled together in the raft, adrift in the stormy darkness.

Grabbing onto the paddles, Jake began rowing them away from the sinking plane. The wind whipped at their hair as the rubber ducky tossed wildly in the choppy waves. The plane disappeared into the depths of the angry sea, now desolate except for the lone rubber raft and its four passengers. In the distance, a giant whirlpool—as if Odysseus' Charybdis had sprung to life—swirled and gurgled, threatening to suck them in. Candide's eyes widened as he spotted the massive maelstrom.

"Row harder!" Pangloss yelled over the storm's fury.

Jake's muscles burned as he battled against the winds and waves driving them toward the maelstrom's gaping maw. A huge wave lifted the rubber ducky airborne. As the rubber ducky crashed back into the water, the impact threw the flight attendant overboard.

Jake handed the paddles to Candide. "Keep us steady," he instructed. The flight attendant, floundering in the water, drifted further from the raft, being drawn helplessly towards the swirling maelstrom.

Before anyone could protest, Jake dove into the churning black water. He swam with powerful strokes toward the flight attendant, fighting against the current dragging them both toward the whirlpool. Just as the vortex was about to pull the flight attendant under, Jake grasped her wrist and yanked her back to the surface. He labored toward the raft, side-stroking through the turbulent water with his left arm while holding the flight attendant with his right. As they reached the rubber raft, Candide and Pangloss grabbed the flight attendant's arms, hauling her aboard. Jake clung to the side, exhausted. Candide reached for Jake's hand, but his grip slipped, and Jake slid back into the rolling waves, too exhausted to swim back to the raft.

"No!" Candide cried out, lunging forward to catch Jake again.

Pangloss seized Candide's shoulder. "It's too late," he said gravely. "This is his fate."

"We have to try!" Candide insisted, shrugging off Pangloss's hand. But Jake had already drifted to the whirlpool. With resignation in his eyes, he circled the drain for one last time, before he was swallowed in the turbulence.

Candide collapsed to his knees, tears mingling with the rain on his cheeks. Pangloss put a comforting hand on his shoulder. After a few moments, Pangloss reminded Candide, "We need to focus on saving ourselves now. Before the storm worsens."

Candide picked up the paddles and steered them away from the terrible vortex. Darkness fell as the storm finally passed. Guided by the moonlight reflecting off the calm waters, Candide paddled them toward a distant shore. The rubber ducky scraped onto the sandy beach, as the sun peeked above the horizon. The flight attendant hopped out without a word. She stripped off her wet uniform down to her red bikini and hurried to a waiting limousine from Club Med.

Candide stared after her in disbelief. "She didn't even say thank you. Or try to help us. She didn't even wave good-bye."

Pangloss sighed. "Some people only think of themselves, I'm afraid. But it's for the best."

Together, they dragged the rubber ducky further up the beach. Candide gazed out at the serene and tranquil waves, silently praying for their lost friend.

The two exhausted men, tired, battered and bruised from their ordeal, trudged up the beach in search of help. As they crested a sandy dune, they spotted a small village in the distance.

"Look—a hospital!" Pangloss exclaimed, pointing to a modest concrete building on the village's outskirts. A worn sign reading "Médecins Sans Frontières" hung crookedly above the entrance.

As they drew nearer, a young man in scrubs hurried out to meet them. "Are you the doctors for the visiting surgical team?" he spoke in rapid French. "We've been expecting you for the cataract operations."

Pangloss gave him a tired nod. "Oui, I am Dr. Pangloss, and this is Dr. Candide."

The man smiled in relief. "Excellent. Please, come with me." He guided them into the cramped, dimly lit hospital. Candide looked around anxiously. The sparse operating theater seemed barely functional, with rusted equipment and frayed privacy curtains. His heart sank as he fully grasped the gravity of the situation. With Jake gone, he was now the Chief of Surgery. It would be all on him. Back home, Candide was a first-year resident who had never performed surgery unsupervised. But here, hundreds were relying on him to restore their sight.

Noticing Candide's wide-eyed expression, Pangloss leaned in and spoke with reassurance, "You've watched the best surgeons in the world operate on YouTube. And I'll be right by your side."

Candide nodded, trying to suppress his nerves. He had to believe he was ready, even if he didn't quite feel it yet. Steeling himself, he followed Pangloss into the operating room to begin preparation for a busy day ahead.

#

The following day, Candide took a deep breath as he gazed at his first patient—a frail elderly man whose cataracts were so advanced they appeared chalky white. A corpulent nurse, her head adorned with a bright yellow bandana, wheeled the patient into the brightly lit surgical room. Candide felt a slight tremor in his hands. He looked up at the grainy YouTube surgical tutorials from eyesurgerycoach.com displayed on the large overhead TV, seeking both inspiration and last-minute instruction. He braced himself for the task ahead. *He can do this. He has to.*

The nurse hoisted the sedated patient onto the operating table, cleansed the right eye with antiseptic, administered the anesthetic eye drop, and covered the eye with a sterile drape, while Candide and Pangloss scrubbed, gowned, and gloved. Picking up the scalpel, Candide leaned in, peering through the microscope, and made the initial incision along the edge of the cornea. Immediately, blood began gushing from the eye, obscuring his view completely.

"Mon Dieu!" Candide cried out in alarm.

Pangloss rushed over with gauze, trying to stanch the bleeding.

"What happened? I barely touched him! Why is he hemorrhaging so badly?" Candide said in a panic.

The elderly man began to stir, mumbling in his local dialect. With the nurse translating, he confessed to using herbal remedies prescribed by the village shaman to ward off evil spirits. These herbs had thinned his blood, reducing the effectiveness of the sedatives.

Candide's face paled at the unforeseen complication. He knew he must remain calm and composed. Time seemed to stretch into eternity before the bleeding finally slowed enough for him to continue. After confirming the patient was adequately sedated, he resumed the surgery, hoping he could still save the man's sight.

Taking another deep breath, Candide steadied his nerves and proceeded to the next step. He carefully inserted the hollow titanium needle into the patient's eye, feeling a subtle vibration in his grip. As irrigation fluid cascaded over the eye, it created ripples and eddies, reminding him of the maelstrom that had engulfed Jake. Positioning the needle's tip against the dense, white cataract, Candide pressed the pedal. The needle was supposed to penetrate and shatter the cataract with ultrasonic vibrations, but instead, it glanced off the cataract's surface as if it were marble.

Furrowing his brow, Candide adjusted the angle of attack and pressed harder into the pedal to increase the power. The lights in the operating room flickered as the power surge taxed the local electrical grid, yet the stubborn cataract remained defiant, mocking his efforts. On the brink of conceding defeat, Candide heard Pangloss's encouraging voice, urging him on.

"You must persist, Candide! This is your destiny—restoring sight to the afflicted!" Encouraged by these words, despite mounting doubts, Candide continued his efforts. He meticulously maneuvered the needle, attacking the stubborn cataract from every angle. As long as the patient's eye was under his care, he felt compelled to keep trying, regardless of the seeming futility.

The needle continued to rebound off the cataract, but Candide pressed on with relentless determination. After over three hours of continuous probing with the vibrating needle, a slip occurred. The needle punctured the iris and created a gaping hole. Candide stopped abruptly, horrified by the damage he had inadvertently caused.

"It's just a small hole in the iris, nothing to worry about!" Pangloss said casually. "The iris isn't critical for vision. Keep going, you're making great progress!"

Despite his reservations, Candide continued as Pangloss instructed, trusting in his mentor's expertise. Hours ticked by without any progress on the stubborn cataract. Then, a calamity struck. The vibrating needle dislodged some vitreous humor, causing the clear gel to drift freely within the eye rather than remaining behind the cataract. A wave of dread washed over Candide as he realized the gravity of his mistake; he might have caused a retinal detachment that could have permanently blinded his patient.

"This is too advanced for my skills," Candide said, moving to withdraw the needle. "I should stop before I do more harm."

Pangloss grabbed his arm, preventing him from stopping. "Don't lose your nerve now! You must have faith in yourself! Vitreous humor is unimportant! Forge ahead and claim victory over that cataract!" Pangloss exhorted.

Candide summoned his last measure of resolve, praying he could salvage the situation despite the prolonged ordeal and numerous setbacks. Although every fiber of his being screamed to stop, he persevered, bolstered by Pangloss's encouragement. He had exerted his utmost effort—pushing, poking, prodding, and pummeling the stubborn cataract—yet it resisted every attempt of the vibrating needle. After twelve grueling hours, a dramatic shift occurred. The cataract, once as solid as marble, began to sink deeper into the eye and then vanished completely, reminding him of Jake's disappearance into the maelstrom. In its absence, an ominous red glow began to emanate from the depths of the eye.

"Eureka!" Pangloss shouted triumphantly. "You've done it, Candide! You have performed your first lens couching, a technique perfected in ancient Egypt. I read about it in my medical school days. You're destined to become a great cataract surgeon!"

It was late evening when the surgery finally ended. Candide was utterly exhausted after hours hunched over the microscope. His right hand was cramped from gripping the needle, his back ached from stiffness, and his neck could barely turn after maintaining the same position for so long. The surgery had been a grueling battle, as if the cataract had given him a beating. He rested his forehead against the microscope, allowing himself a moment to breathe. Then, he leaned back, relieved that the ordeal was over. He removed his surgical gloves, took off the cap from his sweat-drenched hair, and ripped off his blood-stained surgical gown. He hoped the old man would regain some vision after enduring his fumbling attempts.

For now, the long day's work was done. After a good night's rest, he would see how the patient fared in the morning. As Candide finally left the OR, the earth rumbled slightly beneath his weary feet.

Chapter 5

Come, ye philosophers, who cry, 'All's well,'
And contemplate this ruin of a world.
Behold these shreds and cinders of your race,
This child and mother heaped in common wreck,
These scattered limbs beneath the marble shafts—
A hundred thousand whom the earth devours,
Who, torn and bloody, palpitating yet,
Entombed beneath their hospitable roofs,
In racking torment end their stricken lives.
~ Voltaire

The next morning in the clinic, surrounded by the old man's entire family, Candide carefully removed the blood-soaked patch from the old man's eye. He gently pried open the eyelids, crusted with dried blood. The old man flinched at the sudden flood of light and blinked rapidly. As his vision adjusted, a broad grin spread across his dark, weather-beaten face. "I can see!" he exclaimed. "Praise the Lord, I can see again!" He turned to his family, who quickly gathered around, embracing each other as tears of joy streamed down their faces. Rising to his feet, he explored his surroundings with newfound sight. It had been years since he had been able to see well enough to walk on his own.

Candide examined the eye using the slit lamp. The sclera was an angry red, irritated by the blood-thinning herbs the old man had taken. The cornea was notably swollen from the prolonged surgery, and the pupil irregular due to accidental damage to the iris during the operation. Though the result was not aesthetically pleasing, it was functional. Despite the swelling and inflammation, the old man seemed comfortable with his newly restored vision. If the patient could see, that was what mattered the most.

Pangloss stood in the corner with his arms crossed, observing the examination and beaming at his young acolyte. As the family assisted the overjoyed old man out of the room, Pangloss approached Candide and clapped a hand on his shoulder.

"Not bad, my boy. Quite an excellent outcome. On this trip we survived an airplane crash at sea and lost Jake to a whirlpool in the middle of a terrible storm. Without them, though our loss is tragic, you would not have accomplished such a surgical feat. It's all for the best, in the best of all possible worlds."

Pangloss put his arm over Candide's shoulder and continued, "Let's see if we can fix a few more cataracts today, eh? But first we must have breakfast." His easy confidence and paternal pride warmed Candide. He had come far under his mentor's guidance. How many more lives could they transform on this medical mission? It would all work out. He was well on his way to becoming an expert cataract surgeon. Jake would've been proud.

"Yes, let's," Candide replied, filled with optimism, his stomach rumbling. As the words left Candide's mouth, the ground began to shake violently. The walls and floor swayed as seismic waves rippled through the building. Candide and Pangloss strug-gled to keep their footing, bracing themselves against the walls and the doorframe. The shelves crashed to the floor. Books, medical supplies, and equipment scattered. Window glass shattered, and broken pieces of plaster rained down from the ceiling.

"Earthquake!" Pangloss yelled over the din.

They staggered into the hallway, arms shielding their heads from the falling debris. No sooner had they cleared the doorway—the floor gave way. Candide watched in horror as the elderly man, his family, and the entire wing of the hospital fell into a widening chasm right in front of him. Teetering on the crumbling edge, his body lurched back and forth, his arms flailing widely, trying to maintain his balance. As he was about to fall into the chasm, Pangloss seized his arm and yanked him back from the precipice. Nearly overcome, Candide collapsed against his mentor, his breath ragged and knees shaking.

Around them, the walls shuddered and cracked. Half of the building had collapsed. As Pangloss helped Candide to his feet, Candide stared into the deep, jagged pit that had, in an instant, swallowed the old man and his entire family. When Candide looked up, he saw the devastated cityscape: church steeples toppled, and buildings crumbled to dust in quick succession, as if trampled by a mob of invisible giants rampaging through the city. The streets were bent, twisted, and torn apart, as seismic waves rumbled un-derground, one after another, like runaway trains. Panic-stricken city dwellers ran and screamed, their cries for help piercing the chaos. In the distance, sirens wailed relentlessly.

Less than a second later, the remaining half of the building lurched and fell into the chasm, carrying Candide and Pangloss with it. Candide's stomach dropped as he plunged into free fall. Their descent halted with a bone-jarring crash as the building fragment wedged itself deep in a large sinkhole. Dazed, Candide took stock of his surroundings. Dust and debris floated through shafts of daylight piercing the wreckage. Though shaken, he was mostly unharmed, with only a few bruises and superficial cuts. He coughed from the thick dust in the air and blinked to clear it from his eyes. Standing up, he brushed himself off and thought, *where is Pangloss?*

"Pangloss! Pangloss!" Candide shouted, his voice echoing through the unstable cavern, but only dead silence replied. Gingerly, Candide picked his way over mounds of rubble toward the light above. He clambered out of the sinkhole that had engulfed the hospital. As he surveyed the remnants, his heart sank. Where the hospital had once stood, there was an abyss, its edges jagged like the maw of a monstrous creature. Twisted rebar jutted out from piles of concrete and plaster, like the ribs of a great beast laid bare. Candide searched in vain for any signs of life from within the hospital's remains, but heard only dead stillness, an eerie quiet that belied the recent tumult. As he turned back, the city revealed itself as a hellscape of ruin. People were scattered amid the chaos like broken dolls, some stirring weakly, others ominously still.

A scrap of yellow caught his eye—the bandana worn by his nurse. Candide clutched it tightly, overwhelmed by loss. He sat alone amidst the chaos and destruction, hoping that someone—anyone—might emerge from the sink hole. But it soon became clear everyone in the hospital, except him, had perished in the quake. Clutching the nurse's yellow bandana, Candide sat dazed amidst the havoc. How could Pangloss and so many others be gone in an instant? It was inconceivable. He wished Pangloss, Jake, or Cunegonde were by his side. He wished he were back in Boston, still a student at the World's Best Medical School.

A low rumble jolted Candide from his stupor, and the ground began to tremble beneath him. The rumbling quickly escalated into a deafening roar. As Candide turned toward the sound, his heart froze, and his blood ran cold. A massive tsunami was barreling toward him, carrying a chaotic flotsam of debris—shattered ships, crumbled building materials, automobiles, carts, buses, corpses, animal carcasses, fish, sharks, sea kelp—and, to his surprise, the giant rubber ducky bobbing in its foamy wake.

Candide turned and sprinted for his life, scrambling desperately toward the nearest hilltop. He didn't dare look back as the tsunami crashed into the city below. After reaching the hilltop, he watched in horror as the relentless surges inundated half of Port-au-Prince. The hospital was swallowed whole, vanishing beneath the churning waters.

Falling to his knees, Candide's ragged sobs broke the silence of the desolate hilltop. "Pangloss, my friend, my guide—how could this be part of any greater good? You, Jake, and Cunegonde are gone. What am I to do now?" His anguished cries carried across the barren landscape and rose into the sky.

The tsunami had retreated as swiftly as it arrived, dragging with it the remnants of a once-thriving city out to sea and leaving behind a desolate wasteland. Drenched and shivering, Candide sat on the hilltop, watching the scattered survivors emerge from their hiding places. They scurried with a bewildered urgency, like ants in disarray after their anthill had been savagely upturned and stomped by an impetuous child, leaving craters where homes and buildings had once stood.

As the sun set on the cataclysmic day, the sky was ablaze with hues of red and orange, casting an infernal glow over the devastated landscape. Candide, a solitary figure atop the hill, wiped the tears from his cheeks and surveyed the vast, muddy expanse strewn with the debris of shattered lives. The air was filled with the cries of the injured and the mournful wails of those grieving, mingling with the crackling of fires that dotted the ravaged cityscape in a haunting chorus.

Rising to his feet, Candide took a deep breath and descended toward what was left of Port-au-Prince. As he waded through the wreckage in a city that had, earlier that morning, bustled with life, he found himself among other survivors who had miraculously ridden out the dual disasters. They all shared the same blank expression, the same questioning eyes that silently screamed. And in every face, Candide saw reflections of his own loss and confusion.

#

For weeks, Candide wandered through the flooded rubble, dazed and directionless. He trudged through the streets, stumbling over debris in a city now unrecognizable. Dust from the collapsed buildings hung in the air like a dense fog, painting everything in a flat, pewter hue. Tens of thousands of bodies lay scattered, unclaimed, and unburied. The stench permeated the air, making his eyes sting. He covered his nose and mouth with the nurse's yellow bandana.

Candide worked himself to exhaustion, both to help others and to anesthetize his immense grief. Seeking solace, Candide aided the injured as best he could. With rudimentary medical skills, he splinted broken bones, stitched gashes, and amputated crushed limbs. He carried people to makeshift clinics and helped doctors triage the endless waves of victims. At night he collapsed in abandoned buildings, finding rest where he could. He scavenged food from the ruins, accepting whatever meager rations came his way with gratitude.

After toiling through a grueling 36-hour hospital shift, Candide finally allowed himself to break down one night. Overwhelmed by the enormity of the tragedy, he wept into his hands. Entire families had been obliterated, hundreds of thousands orphaned or widowed. He struggled to see how any good could emerge from such devastation. He longed for Pangloss to be by his side. His mentor always had answers, or at least the comforting echo of his philosophy to soften the harsh edges of brutal reality. Pangloss would have spun poetic tales, insisting they lived in the best of all possible worlds, arguing that calamity was merely a necessary step toward some greater, unseen destination. Yet, surrounded by destruction and sorrow, Candide found such assurances empty. The abstract musings of philosophers did little to mend the wounds before him or quell the cries that haunted him every moment.

In a humble hovel, Candide cried until he had no tears left. He lay curled on the hard floor, wishing for sleep's relief. As he drifted off, he felt a hand on his shoulder. An elderly woman stood over him, gazing down with kindness in her eyes. Candide blinked, wondering if he was dreaming. The Old Woman gave him a gentle smile and sat down beside him. In the dim light Candide could see her careworn face and stooped shoulders. She wore simple clothes, stained and dusty from walking through debris.

"Who are you?" he asked. "Why did you come to me tonight?"

The Old Woman's smile widened, revealing stained teeth worn down by time. Her eyes, a cloudy blue, bore the grief of a thousand sorrows. Her skin resembled crumpled parchment that had been smoothed out again. Wisps of silver hair, escaping from her modest bonnet, caught the faint moonlight, casting a halo around her face. She gently rested her workworn, gnarled, but steady hand on Candide's head.

"I'm here at the behest of someone you love dearly. She will be happy to see you are alive and well." The Old Woman continued. "I will come back for you in the morning. Now eat and sleep. Tomorrow your path will become clear." The Old Woman left a wrapped turkey sandwich with mayo and an ice-cold bottle of water by him.

She turned and hobbled off into the night. Candide watched her leave, his heart lighter, but he also wondered—*why did she have only one buttock?*

Chapter 6

When one is loved by a beautiful woman, says the great Zoroaster, one always gets out of trouble in this world. ~ Voltaire

The morning sun crept over the horizon, bathing the countryside in a warm, golden glow. Candide approached a small country house, his heart racing with anticipation, while the Old Woman guided him up the front steps. As promised, the Old Woman returned earlier that morning to Port-au-Prince and retrieved him. She knocked twice and the door creaked open.

Candide's eyes widened as he took in the sight before him. There she was, his Cunegonde, radiant and beautiful as ever. She stood in the doorway, a delicate hand clasped against her chest, her lips parted in a gasp of surprise. Candide froze, overwhelmed by the wave of emotions crashing over him. Relief, joy, longing all mingled together.

Cunegonde let out a cry and rushed into his arms. "Oh Candide, my love! I thought I'd never see you again!" She clung to him, tears of happiness streaming down her cheeks as Candide held her close, stroking her hair. He had dreamt of this moment for so long. "I can't believe you're really here," he murmured. He had traveled so far and endured so much just for this moment—to finally be reunited with his true love.

The Old Woman discreetly slipped away, leaving the two lovers alone. They sat together on the porch, holding hands, as Candide recounted his harrowing adventures—his robbery and the assault by the police upon arriving in Miami, the devastating plane crash, Jake's tragic death, the earthquake and tsunami in Haiti, the loss of Pangloss, and his series of narrow escapes from danger.

Cunegonde told of being expelled from nursing school, becoming pregnant and having a botched abortion. "But I survived, as I knew I must see you again," she said, caressing Candide's cheek.

"But how?" Candide asked, confused. "I was told you died getting an abortion."

Cunegonde shook her head. "Do not believe all you hear. I escaped death to live and find you, my love." She leaned her head against his shoulder. "My dear Candide. But let us not dwell on sorrows of the past. We have been granted a second chance—a rare gift."

She described how she and the Old Woman had rushed to Haiti when they heard Candide was there. When the earthquake occurred, she was desperate to find him.

Candide brushed a strand of hair behind her ear and leaned in to kiss her softly on the lips. "I will never leave your side again," he vowed, holding her close.

The next morning, Cunegonde, Candide and the Old Woman boarded a flight to Miami. Candide received a hero's welcome at the World's Best Eye Institute for his humanitarian efforts in Haiti.

He and Cunegonde moved into a cozy condo on Key Biscayne, looked after by the ever-faithful Old Woman.

Candide resumed his ophthalmology residency at the World's Best Eye Institute, elated to have his beloved Cunegonde by his side once again. Despite the uncertain road ahead, their reunion against all odds was a profound source of joy. For now, that was enough.

However, the loss of Jake was a devastating blow to the Institute. Under his leadership, the World's Best Eye Institute had not only risen to prominence for its cutting-edge research and exceptional patient care but had also become renowned for its humanitarian missions. These efforts provided vital eye care to underserved populations around the globe. His absence was deeply felt across the international community.

Following an exhaustive international search, the Institute's board appointed the Grand Inquisitor, a distinguished ophthalmologist from Guatemala, as Jake's successor. To celebrate his arrival, a welcoming party was held in the grand atrium of the Institute. Candide and Cunegonde, dressed in their finest, attended the event. The atrium was elegantly decorated and brimming with well-dressed guests, all enthusiastic about meeting the new director.

As soon as they entered, the Grand Inquisitor, an imposing man in a stark black suit, immediately noticed Cunegonde's beauty. His expansive girth spoke volumes of his bottomless appetite. He bore a pair of arched eyebrows that could have been mistaken for the wings of a bat. His eyes—tiny, beady, squinting, evaluating and suspecting everyone and everything. His gaze lingered on Cunegonde, and Candide felt a slight unease. They approached him with polite smiles, as Candide introduced himself and Cunegonde.

"What an exquisite creature you are," he said, taking her hand. "I simply must have you as my personal secretary." He held Cunegonde's hand and gave her a suggestive look.

Cunegonde lowered her eyes demurely. "You honor me, sir. I gratefully accept."

Privately, she and Candide exchanged amused glances. The vainglorious Inquisitor was clearly besotted with her.

Taken aback by the intensity of the new director's attention toward Cunegonde, Candide felt a protective instinct surge within him. As the Inquisitor clasped Cunegonde's hand, Candide responded with a polite demeanor that masked his discomfort, saying, "I am sure she will prove to be an invaluable asset to your team."

The Grand Inquisitor shifted his gaze from Cunegonde to Candide, offering an approving nod. "Ah, the renowned Dr. Candide," he remarked, taking a deep bow with a flourish of his hand, nearly toppling over. "Your work in Haiti has captured the attention of the medical community. We anticipate great contributions from you."

Candide inclined his head, acknowledging the compliment but wary of the undercurrents in the conversation. If the position gave Cunegonde access and influence, they would humor him. Their priority was being together and supporting each other.

At the party, Candide and Cunegonde met Martin, a fellow resident at the Institute. Though close in age to Candide, Martin's life experience made him look far older. His eyes were a piercing shade of green that seemed almost unnatural against his dark, sun-worn skin. His afro was an unruly shock of salt and pepper. The strands rebelled against any attempt at taming. Martin's frame was lean, almost ascetic. He moved with an economical grace, each motion hinting at an efficiency honed through years of hardship and survival.

Martin grew up in poverty, raised by a single mother in Chicago's roughest housing project. He was one of fourteen children, each with a different absent father. As a child, Martin witnessed constant violence, crime, and drug addiction. Most of his friends died young or ended up in prison.

At seventeen, Martin enlisted in the Marines to escape. As a combat medic, Martin was stationed around the world. He saw firsthand the ravages of war, poverty, disease, and human cruelty. While deployed in Afghanistan, he lost his legs to an IED. After being honorably discharged, Martin persevered through college, medical school, and finally his ophthalmology residency at the Institute.

Martin's childhood and military service left him with a bleak, cynical view of humanity. Yet Candide and Cunegonde found his life story fascinating. They sensed his inner goodness despite the darkness he exuded.

As the evening wore on, the chatter of guests grew to a hum, punctuated by the clinking of glasses and the distant melody of a string quartet. Candide listened to Martin's somber tales, finding similarities to his own recent experiences.

With the ice cubes of his drink rattling against the crystal tumbler, Martin sipped and looked around. His gaze grew distant as he spoke. "You see the world through rose-tinted glasses," he said, his voice roughened from years of exposure to desert sands and urban smog. "Life, as I've come to know it, is an endless cycle of misery. Human nature is inherently flawed."

Candide shook his head with a smile. "Nonsense, dear Martin! The world is full of wonders and good people striving to make a difference. Just look around you—this Institute is a testament to the potential of human kindness and ingenuity."

Martin let out a dry, derisive chuckle. "This? This is just a façade—a glimmering veneer that masks underlying corruption and self-interest. You think these doctors are here out of altruism? No, they chase fame, fortune, and bolster their insatiable egos."

Cunegonde, who had been quietly observing the exchange, chimed in, "Surely, Martin, there must be some hope left in you? Not everyone can be as you describe."

"Hope?" Martin quirked an eyebrow and stared into his drink. "Hope is the carrot dangled in front of the downtrodden to keep them in line. It's an illusion. In my experience, people are driven by fear or desire—nothing more noble than that."

The room hushed, as the Grand Inquisitor took the stage to eulogize Jake and share his vision. "Ladies and gentlemen, we gather tonight to honor the memory of Jake Anabaptiste—a man who embodied the principles of diversity, equity, and inclusion. It is in this spirit that I wish to speak to you about a vision—a vision for our future. We stand at the precipice of a new era—an era where the shadows of our past mistakes must be acknowledged and addressed. We are gathered here today not just in memory of our dear colleague, Jake, but to affirm our commitment to a brighter, fairer future."

He paused, his gaze sweeping over the audience before continuing. "Diversity is not just an ideal; it is the very fabric that weaves our society together. It is the spectrum of experiences, cultures, and voices that enrich our collective human spirit . . . "

The Grand Inquisitor vowed to address historical injustices and fight systemic racism. Candide found the speech inspiring, though Martin remained skeptical of the Inquisitor's intentions. Martin watched impassively as the Grand Inquisitor spoke with eloquence of equity and inclusion, amused by the Inquisitor's flowery promises that rang hollow to him. He had seen too much hypocrisy from powerful figures who espoused idealism while pursuing their own agendas. Too many promises made, too few fulfilled.

Candide beamed as the Inquisitor spoke, his face radiating optimism. To him, the speech was a manifestation of the Panglossian ideals, proof of progress toward a utopia of fairness and enlightenment. He smiled, imagining Pangloss's praise for the Inquisitor's vision of equity and inclusion at the Institute. Candide envisioned a bright future for the WBEI under their new director, and with Cunegonde by his side, he felt hopeful about what lay ahead.

Yet Martin was biting his lips, viewing the Inquisitor's grand vision as nothing more than a smokescreen. His thoughts were bitter, but Candide's smiling enthusiasm gave him pause. Perhaps the young man's buoyant spirit stemmed from a place of goodness rather than ignorance. In that moment, Martin decided to temper his cynicism. He resolved not to dampen Candide's high hopes, though he remained unconvinced himself. Despite coming from different worlds, Martin felt a sense of kinship with this optimistic youth. For now, he would hold off on judging him.

After the speech, Candide approached Martin to resume their earlier conversation. Though naturally optimistic, Candide's experiences in Haiti had confronted him with profound suffering that once shook his faith in Pangloss's philosophy. He was eager to learn from Martin's perspective. "My friend, I must confess that the earthquake in Haiti made me reconsider," Candide started. "I witnessed such devastation and loss of life. It challenged my belief that all is for the best in this world."

Martin concurred. "I witnessed similar tragedies as a battle-field medic. Such experiences mark a man forever."

"Yet I cannot abandon hope," Candide continued. "Surely there is some greater purpose, some way to make sense of such tragedy?"

Martin sighed. "Friend, I admire your spirit. But for me, the cruelty of this world defies reason. I can only accept it and do what little I can to help."

Struggling to reconcile their views, Candide furrowed his brow. Yet Martin's honesty resonated with him.

"I don't share your disillusionment," Candide said finally. "But I respect your perspective. Perhaps between hope and resignation lies wisdom."

Martin gave Candide a faint smile. "Well said. I'm glad we could discuss this with civility."

"I'm glad we had a chance to talk." Candide gave Martin a warm smile in return, as they walked to the exit. "It's not often I meet someone who speaks so plainly."

"Likewise," Martin replied. "Most cling to optimism despite the darkness in this world. But you listened and did not judge me harshly for my cynicism."

"We all see through our own lens," Candide said. "Yours was forged in great hardship. Who am I to dismiss it?"

Martin nodded. "I hope we talk again soon."

"Absolutely! I feel I've made a true friend tonight."

With a smile and handshake, they parted ways into the night. Candide and Cunegonde strode happily back to their condo, heartened to find a kindred spirit in an unlikely place.

#

Candide arrived at the Institute the next day and was surprised to see a notice posted on the main bulletin board which read:

Under DiversiCare, the new DEI policy, all staff and residents at the WBEI are required to attend sensitivity and inclusivity training sessions.

"What's all this about?" Candide asked a passerby.

The woman rolled her eyes. "It's part of the Grand Inquisitor's new policy. Mandatory for everyone."

Candide blinked in surprise but shrugged it off. He trusted the Grand Inquisitor's vision. If this training was required, it would serve the greater good.

Chapter 7

It is dangerous to be right in matters where established men are wrong. ~ Voltaire

Candide stared at the walls of the training room, his eyes widened at the bold slogans shouting, *Embrace Diversity! Foster Equity! Promote Inclusion! Trump Racism!* and *Trust DiversiCare!* He could scarcely contain his excitement. This was his chance to change the world!

Beside him, Martin slouched in his chair, regarding the decor with a cynical sneer. Cunegonde tapped away on her phone, oblivious to the motivational messages around her.

Dr. Equitya Whitewash, the DEI trainer, marched to the front of the room with a confident sway, dressed in a tailored Mao suit with a red armband and a Mao cap. "Welcome, everyone, to the sensitivity and inclusivity training!" she announced, beaming and extending her arms in a welcoming gesture. "It is my honor to lead this inaugural DEI class as part of the DiversiCare initiative at the Institute."

Standing at the forefront of the room, Dr. Equitya Whitewash filled it with an air of saccharine authority. She was a tall woman. Her skin was a rich, deep brown, eyes, large expressive pools of obsidian that twinkled. Equitya's hair was a spectacular afro crowning her head like a halo of tightly coiled black springs. Her grin, as she greeted them, was so wide it split her face in two, revealing her perfect white teeth.

"Now, before we begin, let's recite the *Pledge of Allegiance to DiversiCare*. Please stand," she commanded.

With her right hand over her heart and her gaze fixed on the portrait of the Grand Inquisitor on the back wall, Dr. Whitewash's contralto voice resonated through the conference room with a dark, rhythmic cadence:

I pledge allegiance to DiversiCare,
And to the inclusive policies for which it stands.
One health Initiative, under the Grand Inquisitor, indivisible,
With equitable care and mandatory sensitivity training for all.

"Thank you. Please be seated. Let's begin."

Candide sat straight, pen poised over paper, ready to absorb every pearl of wisdom. Martin stifled a yawn. Cunegonde glanced up briefly before returning to her phone.

"Comrades and patriots, today, we'll explore the intricacies of gender pronouns," Dr. Whitewash continued. "It's essential we understand and validate everyone's chosen pronouns."

Candide nodded with enthusiasm, his pen dancing across the paper as he scribbled down every detail. This was the moment he had been waiting for—the key to unlocking a brighter future for the world.

Martin leaned back, muttering, "Riveting stuff, truly."

Cunegonde scrolled on her phone.

Dr. Whitewash held up a card reading "Ze/Zir." "Let's practice using these pronouns in a sentence," she said brightly.

Candide's hand shot up. "I met zir at the diversity rally last week. Ze gave a rousing speech on inclusion!"

"Excellent, Candide!" Dr. Whitewash said. She turned expectantly to the others.

"Oh, right. Ze seems very nice," Cunegonde said halfheartedly, not looking up from her phone.

Martin smirked. "I do hope zir remembers to pick up milk on the way home."

Candide beamed, thrilled at the chance to change the world, one pronoun at a time.

Dr. Whitewash clapped her hands with exaggerated enthusiasm. "Wonderful! Now, class, let's move on to neopronouns."

She held up a card reading "Ey/Em" while displaying her gleaming white teeth with a wide grin.

Candide's hand shot up again. "I ran into em at the coffee shop. Ey had just ordered an oat milk latte."

Dr. Whitewash nodded with approval. "Very good, Candide! Let's keep practicing."

She cycled through more neopronouns - xe/xem, ae/aer, and ve/ver. With each one, Candide eagerly provided an example, while Martin stifled yawns and Cunegonde scrolled on her phone.

"Remember, using someone's correct pronouns validates their identity," Dr. Whitewash said with theatrical earnestness.

"Of course!" Candide exclaimed. "What an impact we can have by simply adapting our language."

Martin leaned over to Cunegonde. "Wake me up when she gets to pronouns for furniture and houseplants," he muttered.

Cunegonde glanced up briefly, suppressing a smirk, before returning to her phone once more.

"That's enough for today," Dr. Whitewash finally said. "We'll reconvene tomorrow for a lesson on microaggressions and triggers. Please review the relevant material and the assigned readings from the *Little Red Book,* a collection of the Grand Inquisitor's quotations on DEI. You will find them as enlightening as I do. It's my daily catechism. Remember, the path to true diversity is never-ending. Class dismissed."

Candide gathered his notes, brimming with inspiration. He felt empowered with his newfound knowledge to make a meaningful impact and transform the world for the better!

Martin stretched slowly. "Well, that was truly life changing."

Cunegonde stood up, eyes glued to her phone. "Mmhmm, fascinating," she murmured, already scrolling away.

#

The next day, Candide's enthusiasm was palpable as Dr. Whitewash began the next portion of the training on microaggressions and triggers.

"Remember, even small slights can cause harm," the doctor spoke with gravitas. "We must avoid microaggressions at all costs."

Candide nodded vigorously, scribbling notes. Meanwhile, Martin stifled a yawn.

Dr. Whitewash held up a poster titled "Examples of Microaggressions" which listed statements like "You speak so articulately!" and "Where are you really from?"

"Avoid these at all costs!" She raised a fist high above her head for emphasis.

"Of course," Candide replied with utmost earnestness. "I will be mindful going forward."

Cunegonde glanced up briefly before returning to her phone, oblivious to the discussion.

"It's also crucial that we avoid potential triggers," Dr. Whitewash continued. "We must provide ample trigger warnings." She held up another poster listing various potential triggers from spiders to loud noises.

"I'll be sure to provide warnings for any of these," Candide declared.

Martin leaned over to Cunegonde again. "Let me know if she mentions trigger warnings for tedium," he muttered. "That's my trigger."

Cunegonde's eyes remained fixed on her phone.

"Excellent!" Dr. Whitewash said. "Remember, we must create safe, inclusive spaces for all. I'm so pleased you're embracing these values."

Candide beamed, bursting with idealism. "Of course! Together we can make the world a better place, eliminating one microaggression at a time."

Martin stifled another yawn. "Fascinating," he murmured under his breath. "Simply fascinating."

Martin's eyes glazed over as Dr. Whitewash droned on about microaggressions and triggers. He leaned over to Cunegonde. "At what point does coddling become more harmful than these trivial slights?" he whispered.

Cunegonde glanced up briefly from her phone and gave a small shrug before returning her attention to the screen.

"We must provide warnings anytime, anywhere," she declared. "No potential trigger should go unaddressed."

Candide's pen flew across his notebook. "Of course! Leaving someone unwarned is an act of violence itself!"

Martin leaned towards Cunegonde, whispering under his breath. "I'd like to warn her about the triggers of condescension and absurdity."

Eyes glued to her phone, Cunegonde didn't react, while Martin sighed and slumped back in his seat.

Dr. Whitewash paused her lecture to pass out pins reading, "I Bravely Avoid Microaggressions," instructing everyone to always wear them.

As Candide eagerly fastened his pin to his lapel, Martin rolled his eyes. "I'll be sure to wear this as I micro-analyze every interaction for the slightest unintended offense," he grumbled.

Candide beamed, not detecting Martin's sarcasm. "What a wonderful idea! A visible sign of our commitment to equity."

Martin sighed again and glanced at his watch, wondering when this charade would finally end.

Cunegonde stifled another yawn and glanced at her watch yet again. The morning's diversity training was dragging on, and her attention was clearly elsewhere.

Meanwhile, Candide's hand shot eagerly into the air, not waiting to be called on, before he launched into sharing his experience. "I once encountered microaggression when someone used a gendered pronoun to address me," he declared fervently. "I believe it's essential to create safe spaces for everyone, free from any potential harm or discomfort."

Martin let out an exaggerated sigh, not bothering to hide his cynicism. "Ah yes, the dreaded *gendered pronoun*," he muttered just loud enough for Candide and Cunegonde to hear. "Truly a matter of global importance."

Candide chose not to engage with the sarcastic quip, staying focused on the important topic at hand. He discussed passionately the significance of pronouns and the power of validation, highlighting the importance of respecting individual identities and promoting inclusivity in every conversation.

Cunegonde stifled a laugh at Martin's remark before returning her gaze to her watch, noticing they still had 50 more minutes before freedom.

Martin leaned back in his chair, wondering if Candide would ever realize that coddling people from the slightest perceived slights did more harm than good. But Candide seemed too starry-eyed, too convinced he was making the world a better place.

With another sigh, Martin resigned himself to enduring the rest of this absurd charade.

Dr. Whitewash clapped her hands together, cutting off Candide's enthusiastic monologue. "Wonderful sharing, everyone! Now let's move on to our next activity."

She gestured to a large poster board at the front of the room bearing the title of "Implicit Bias Bingo." "I'm passing out cards with common bias-related terms. Mark off any squares that resonate with your experiences, and let's see who gets to BINGO first!" As she handed out the cards, Candide eagerly scanned his, eyes lighting up at words like "unconscious bias," "intersectionality," and "privileged fragility." He poised his marker above the card, ready to start making X's. Martin glanced down at his own card, unable to hold back an eyeroll. He uncapped his marker and mindlessly started marking "BINGO" diagonally across the card.

"Bingo," he announced flatly, without even reading what he was marking off.

Candide shot him an offended look. "Martin! You can't just mark any random squares. This is about self-reflection and identifying real instances of bias."

Martin shrugged. "My apologies. I'll be sure to take this very seriously."

Meanwhile, Cunegonde had tuned out again, idly doodling in the margins of her untouched bingo card.

Candide eagerly raised his hand, waving it to get the trainer's attention. "I have a story about unconscious bias!" he exclaimed. "Just yesterday, I assumed the janitor was a man, but when I greeted her, she corrected me about her gender. It was an important reminder about my own implicit biases."

He glowed with pride at his self-awareness, while Martin blinked rapidly to suppress another eyeroll.

"Well done, Candide!" Dr. Whitewash said. "Identifying moments like that is key." She launched into a lecture about recognizing microaggressions, with Candide listening intently and taking meticulous notes. Martin, meanwhile, scribbled sarcastic commentary in the margins of his notebook, snickering under his breath.

Cunegonde had abandoned any pretense of paying attention. She was fully immersed in sketching an elaborate dress, occasionally glancing at her watch as if willing the time to pass faster.

"Alright, let's move on to discussing safe spaces," Dr. Whitewash continued. Candide's hand shot up again. "I just want to say, this training has given me so much hope! I feel inspired to make the world a more understanding place."

Martin shook his head and muttered to no one in particular, "Such blind optimism in the face of bureaucratic nonsense."

Cunegonde sat doodling as Dr. Whitewash rambled about "allyship" and "speaking your truth." Candide was still furiously taking notes. Martin had resorted to playing hangman on his notepad to pass the time.

Cunegonde glanced at the clock for the hundredth time. Still 40 minutes left before their lunch break. She yawned and shifted in her seat, her attention drifting around the room. Her gaze landed on a poster that read *Equity! It Takes All of Us!* in bold rainbow letters. Cunegonde frowned slightly. She raised her hand.

"Yes, Cunegonde?" Dr. Whitewash said.

"I was just wondering," Cunegonde began, "is any of this actually going to help us provide better healthcare?"

"Well, you see, by focusing on concepts like diversity, equity and inclusion, we create a more welcoming environment for people of all backgrounds," she explained. "This indirectly improves patient care and outcomes."

"I just mean, shouldn't we be learning skills that directly impact patients, like new medical procedures or technology?" Cunegonde pressed.

Dr. Whitewash gave her a patient, condescending smile. "I understand your perspective. But these issues are equally important for providing compassionate care. A diverse, equitable, inclusive workplace is better for everyone."

Martin couldn't help but scoff, "Ah, the *indirectly improving patient care* trick. That's a new one."

Dr. Whitewash turned to look at him, her eyebrows raised. "I'm sorry, do you have something to add, Martin?"

"Oh, nothing at all," Martin replied casually. "Just appreciating the creativity of your argument. 'Indirectly improving care,' well, that's one I haven't heard before."

Dr. Whitewash pursed her lips. "This training is designed by experts to foster an environment of inclusion. But I suppose you know better?"

Martin held up his hands in mock surrender. "Far be it from me to question the experts. Please, continue enlightening us."

Dr. Whitewash gave Martin one more stern look before turning back to the class. "As I was saying, an inclusive workplace has a positive ripple effect on patient care and satisfaction. Now, let's move on to unpacking unconscious bias . . ."

As Dr. Whitewash launched into a detailed explanation of implicit bias and microaggressions, Cunegonde discreetly pulled out her phone and started texting under the table.

Martin leaned over and whispered, "Planning your escape route?"

Cunegonde smirked. "I have a mani/pedi appointment in 20 minutes that I simply cannot miss."

"Well, in that case, duty calls," Martin replied. "No lecture should stand in the way of proper nail care."

"Exactly!" Cunegonde said. "I mean, just look at these cuticles." She held out her hands with fingers extended. "They're hideous, right?"

Martin nodded solemnly. "A true tragedy. The only solution is an immediate extraction from this training."

"Glad you understand," Cunegonde winked, gathering up her things. Just as Dr. Whitewash turned around, Cunegonde was preparing to leave.

"Excuse me, where are you going?" she asked sharply. "We're only halfway done." Cunegonde flashed her a dazzling smile. "So sorry, but I have a critical nail appointment that simply cannot wait." And with that, she breezed out of the room, leaving Dr. Whitewash momentarily speechless.

Martin chuckled and shook his head. "Never stand between a woman and her manicure."

Dr. Whitewash cleared her throat and attempted to regain control of the room. "Okay everyone, let's get back on track, shall we?" she said, holding up a stack of flashcards with various pronouns written on them. "I want to spend the rest of our time today going through these LGBTQ pronouns to ensure everyone feels comfortable using them."

With a near superhuman effort, Martin suppressed another eyeroll. *More nonsense!* But the sooner they got through this, the sooner he could escape. His prosthetic legs were growing numb from sitting too long.

Dr. Whitewash went through the flashcards one by one, explaining the proper usage of pronouns like ze/zir, ey/em, and ae/aer. Martin tuned her out, his mind drifting to the bottle of whiskey waiting for him at home.

"Now I want everyone to practice using these pronouns in sentences," Dr. Whitewash said brightly, her eyes scanning the room. "How about you, Martin? Can you give us an example with ze/zir?"

Martin blinked, caught off guard. "Uh, hmm . . . let's see . . ." He racked his brain, grasping for any sentence that would satisfy her. "Ze went to the liquor store to replenish zir whiskey supply after a long day spent in a mind-numbing DEI training session," he said flatly.

Dr. Whitewash pursed her lips. "Yes, very good, Martin. Though perhaps next time you could use a more . . . positive example."

"Duly noted." Martin gave her a wry smile and pointed at her with a finger gun.

The trainer continued around the room, eliciting painfully awkward example sentences from each participant. Martin tuned out again, contemplating how much whiskey it would take to erase this experience from his memory.

At last, Dr. Whitewash wrapped up the session. "Excellent work today, everyone. I hope you all feel more enlightened and empowered to use proper pronouns."

Martin barely suppressed a derisive snort. As he gathered his belongings to leave, he whispered under his breath, "The only thing I feel empowered to do right now is pour myself a stiff drink."

"For tomorrow's session, we'll delve into gender identity and sexual orientation terminology," Dr. Whitewash continued.

"Please review the relevant material and complete your daily cate-chism from the Grand Inquisitor's *Little Red Book*. Thank you all for coming today. See you tomorrow!"

With that, she dismissed the group. Candide nearly bounced out of his seat, eager to apply his new knowledge. Pangloss would've been proud.

Chapter 8

*Those who can be convinced of absurdities can be
convinced to commit atrocities. ~ Voltaire*

The Old Woman blinked her eyes open, the blurry world swimming into focus for a moment before dissolving back into indistinct shadows and shapes.

"Madam, can you hear me?" A disembodied voice floated to her. She struggled to reply, her throat dry and raspy.

"The surgery was a success. You should experience significantly improved vision once you've recovered."

She squinted at the figure looming over her, clutching at the thin hospital gown draped over her bony frame. Her eyes blazed as if she'd stared straight into a solar eclipse—or the harsh glow of the overhead fluorescent light. Tears leaked down her cheeks. *This isn't right.* She could barely make out the nurse's face, her features a messy smear. She blinked again and again, panic bubbling in her chest as the room remained stubbornly out of focus. *Think.* What had the ophthalmologist said before the surgery? Something about removing only half the cataract in each eye to meet their diversity quotas. Still in the fog of anesthesia, she could not exactly recall. "I can't see," she croaked. "Everything's still blurry." The Old Woman waved her hands in front her eyes.

"That's perfectly normal after such a procedure," the nurse said brightly. "Your vision will improve over the next few days."

Helping the Old Woman out of the WBEI and into a taxi, Cunegonde's heart ached at the sight of her distressed, half-blind companion. *What happened?* Cunegonde thought to herself. From her experience working at the WBEI, cataract surgery was usually successful and routine. For the past year, the Old Woman's vision had deteriorated to the point she could no longer drive and was having difficulty housekeeping for Candide and Cunegonde. She was seen at the WBEI and was diagnosed as having cataracts in both eyes. Cataract surgeries were recommended to restore her sight. That was a few weeks ago.

When they arrived home, Cunegonde sat the Old Woman down on the sofa with a cup of tea and a blanket, promising to return shortly. The Old Woman clutched at her arm, panic in her clouded eyes. "Don't leave me alone, please. I can't see!"

Cunegonde found Candide in the study. With one glance, Candide was concerned. The Old Woman's eyes looked far worse than the eye of the old man he operated on in Haiti. He called Martin. After hanging up, Candide said to Cunegonde, "Martin will meet us at the WBEI as soon as we get there."

"We go now, all of us," Cunegonde said as they went to get the Old Woman.

One hour later at the WBEI, Martin examined the old woman's eye at the slit lamp. "The surgeon removed only half of the cataract in each eye. Her eyes are inflamed. The corneas are swollen, and the pressure is elevated in both eyes."

"What should be done?" Cunegonde asked, filled with concern.

"The remaining half of the cataracts must be removed soon. Otherwise, there could be permanent vision loss."

"Whose crazy idea is this, removing only half of a cataract?" Candide questioned.

"I could only guess," Martin said.

"I know where to get some answers. Follow me." Cunegonde led the way, with Candide and Martin close behind.

Cunegonde slammed the door open. The Grand Inquisitor was sitting behind a large oak desk and Dr. Whitewash was standing next to him pointing to the computer screen in front of them. They looked up at the three intruders, as if they had materialized in front of them out of thin air.

"What can I do for you two gentleman and this fine lady?" The Grand Inquisitor addressed them in a cold tone.

Candide spoke up first, "We need to discuss why only half of the cataracts were removed in our housekeeper. Her vision is worse now than before surgery. She is practically blind and in pain all the time."

The Grand Inquisitor regarded them with a steely gaze. "I see you're dissatisfied with our diversity and inclusion efforts. Unfortunately, sacrifices must be made to right historical injustices."

"Injustices?" Candide exploded. "This is cruelty, plain and simple. No one should suffer like this for the sake of any ideals."

Dr. Whitewash sniffed. "I hardly expect privileged individuals like yourselves to understand. Equity is never convenient or painless."

"Undo this," Cunegonde, nearly screaming. "Fix her eyes immediately!"

The Grand Inquisitor smirked, enjoying their distress. "I'm afraid that won't be possible. As regrettable as the situation is, we must hold fast to our principles. As you know, historically whites underwent cataract surgery at twice the frequency as other minority groups."

Equitya Whitewash added, "Our policy is a necessary step to address historical imbalances in healthcare. Sacrifices must be made for the greater good."

Martin retorted, "Sacrifices? More like medical malpractice in the name of equity. This is inhumane. Animals get better eye care than this"

Exasperated, Cunegonde jumped in with a plaintive voice. "This policy is not helping anyone. It's causing harm, plain and simple. This poor old lady needs help, and don't give us more pontification on the merits of DEI."

The Grand Inquisitor, self-satisfied, interjected, "Your concerns do not alter our commitment to DEI. In fact, you should know that both Candide and Martin have failed the mandatory DEI competency exam."

Candide, bewildered, asked, "Why did I fail? I had a perfect score."

The Grand Inquisitor sneered, "Candide, you're white. That's why you failed. And Martin, you scored a big fat zero."

Candide, confused, looked from face to face. "So, I failed because of my race? Isn't that racism?"

Equitya Whitewash chimed in, "It's about equity, Candide. We have to ensure that the right people pass. Equity trumps racism."

Puzzled, Candide questioned, "How about diversity and inclusion? Where do they fit in?"

Equitya countered, "Equity trumps both diversity and inclusion, which in turn trump racism. Between inclusion and diversity, it's a toss-up. On even days of the month, inclusion trumps diversity; vice versa on odd days."

"Then where do we whites fit in?" Candide, now baffled, asked.

The Grand Inquisitor stood up and declared, "Under DiversiCare, there is no place for whites. Historically, whites, which you and Martin represent, are the oppressors due to your white privilege. You are an affront to the oppressed, like Dr. Equitya Whitewash, a Nigerian princess, and me, a proud Guatemalan descendant of the conquistadors."

Equitya strode forward until she loomed over Candide. "For too long, your kind have hoarded power and opportunities while oppressing minorities. Now the tables have turned, and you will get exactly what you deserve."

Martin muttered, "Guess who is oppressing whom here."

Candide, now completely astounded, argued, "How about Martin? He's black and he's darker than any of us."

The Grand Inquisitor scolded, "Martin's score is so low on the DEI test, he is practically white, only his skin is black. Under DiversiCare, you and Martin will need remediation."

"And what is that?" Candide cried.

"*What that means* . . . " The Grand Inquisitor stated with indifference, " . . . is that *you*—Candide—are to be burned at the stake and Martin to be flogged in public."

Equitya Whitewash whispered into the Grand Inquisitor's ear reminding him in the 21st century it was no longer customary to burn or flog infidels.

The Grand Inquisitor cleared his throat. "Taking into consideration your service to humanity in Haiti, Candide, and your sacrifice for our country, Martin, I hereby commute your sentences. Candide, you are excommunicated—I mean fired. And Martin, you will be assigned to DEI training for the duration of your residency at the WBEI."

Candide in shock, gasped, "You've got to be kidding me."

Martin, "Just shoot me."

Cunegonde asked, "What about me? Did I pass? I'm white"

The Grand Inquisitor smirked. "Oh, Cunegonde, you passed with flying colors. You're exactly the kind of person I want to keep close. As my personal secretary, I have many projects in mind for us to work closely together."

Cunegonde was dumbfounded. She hadn't answered a single question on the exam, yet she was the one deemed competent.

"I don't know what depraved plans you have for me," Cunegonde spat, "but I want no part in them. Consider this my resignation."

In a fit of rage, Candide swung his fist at the Grand Inquisitor, striking him on the temple with a sickening crunch. The man collapsed like a limp puppet, eyes rolling back. Martin immediately jumped over the desk to check on the Grand Inquisitor. He raised the man's eyelids and shone a penlight to check the pupils. "Call an ambulance! There is not a moment to lose!"

Later that evening, the Grand Inquisitor succumbed to his head injury, leaving Miami and the Eye Institute in a state of shock. The police charged Candide with second degree murder—Candide had become a fugitive.

#

Late at night, somewhere in Miami, Candide paced in the small motel room, adrenaline still pumping through his veins. In a fit of anger, he had acted rashly. But now, as the reality of his situation sank in, he was overcome with a mix of fear and regret.

While the Old Woman was sitting in a lounge chair, Cunegonde sat on the edge of the bed, face pale, but resolute. "We cannot stay here," she said. "It's only a matter of time before they find us."

Candide stopped pacing and looked at her, his eyes wild with panic. "What do you suggest? I'm a murderer now—I've killed a man! A high priest, no less."

"No," Cunegonde replied firmly. "You acted in defense of my honor in the heat of passion. It was not premeditated." A knock at the door made them both jump. Martin came in, looking over his shoulder. "No time to waste," he said. "I have procured a boat. Are you ready?"

Candide nodded, though his hands trembled. "Yes," he whispered, grasping at the lifeline Martin offered. "But where can we go?"

"South," Martin replied with an air of determination. "The Caribbean. Somewhere beyond the reach of DEI."

Cunegonde grabbed a small bag hastily packed with essentials and helped the Old Woman to her feet. The foursome crept out of the motel and into the sultry Miami night, sticking to the shadows as they made their way to the marina where Martin's boat was moored.

Under the light of a half-moon, the boat cut smoothly through the dark waters, as the lights of Miami faded into the horizon, putting more distance between the fugitives and the city. Candide stood at the bow, one arm wrapped around Cunegonde as they gazed ahead into the night. "Do you think we did the right thing?" Candide asked softly.

Cunegonde considered for a moment. "I think we did the only thing we could," she replied. "Staying would have destroyed us."

Candide nodded, drawing her closer. Behind them, Martin and the Old Woman sat hunched against the chill. Martin gazed the horizon with a grim scowl, while the Old Woman dozed off, the boat's gentle rocking lulling her into a fitful sleep.

After some time, Martin got up and joined Candide at the fore. "Cuba awaits," he said with a wry smile. "Who knows if we'll find any more wisdom or truth there than what we left. But I suppose it's worth a shot."

Candide met his friend's gaze. "It has to be better than what we left," he said. "I wonder what Pangloss would say?" As the first pink light of dawn broke, the outline of an island emerged from the mist. In the distance, a giant rubber ducky's head bobbed as it drifted over the horizon to meet the rising sun.

Chapter 9

I have wanted to kill myself a hundred times, but somehow I am still in love with life. This ridiculous weakness is perhaps one of our more stupid melancholy propensities, for is there anything more absurd than to wish to carry continually a burden which one always wants to throw on the ground? To hold one's existence in horror, and yet to cling to it? To fondle the serpent which devours us till it has eaten our hearts away? ~ the Old Woman

The Old Woman stirred from her restless slumber, momentarily unsure of her surroundings. She stood up and gazed out at the rolling waves, her knuckles whitening around the railing. Sixteen years old again, she remembered salt spray stinging her eyes as the pirates swarmed aboard her family's yacht. Screams rent the air, silenced one by one until only she remained, trembling amidst the corpses of the crew and her loved ones. Rough hands had seized her arms, dragging her aboard the pirate ship. The captain strode forward, greed and cruelty etched into his features, as weathered as the timbers of his ship.

"A prize beyond price," he rasped, grasping her chin. She jerked away, defiance in her eyes. The back of his hand cracked across her cheek, splitting her lip.

"Spirit, she has," he chuckled. "It will make breaking her all the sweeter."

The Old Woman shuddered, trying to banish the ghosts of memory. Many times, she had stood at death's door, longing for the release into oblivion. Yet something within her had endured, a flame to warm her on the coldest nights, a light to guide her way. She gazed at Candide, Cunegonde, and Martin, her newfound family. The Old Woman smiled, wiping a tear from her eye. In their company, she had found a home.

Taking a deep breath to steady her nerves, she prepared to share her story. Even after so many years, the act still filled her with trepidation. But she braced herself, gazing into the eyes of her companions, drawing strength from the compassion reflected there.

She swallowed hard and began to speak . . . "I was an only child, born to wealthy parents who had long given up the hope of having a child of their own. To them, I was a miracle. I was raised in the lap of luxury and privilege. My parents loved sailing and every summer we would take our yacht to various parts of the world. For my sixteenth birthday, we explored the Mediterranean. Later, as we sailed through the Suez Canal into the Red Sea, pirates hijacked our yacht."

"I was taken first to Morocco, which was in the middle of civil war, where the pirate captain who captured me was killed. I was rescued by an Italian man, who was gay, He sold me to a wealthy man in Algiers, where the plague broke out, killing him. I then was sold to a caravan of nomads. I traveled in their custody to Tunis, then to Tripoli, from Tripoli to Alexandria, then to Istanbul, where I was trafficked as a sex slave."

"A Turkish tycoon later bought me to be part of his harem. He had a large country estate in Azov where he kept his concubines. Soon after, the estate was attacked by an army of thugs working for a Russian oligarch. They raped and massacred the women in the harem. I alone survived, concealed among the dead. A drunken Russian thug shot off my buttock, as he machine-gunned wildly into the corpses where I was hiding. With one buttock missing, I managed to escape."

"I traveled and worked all over Europe from Moscow to Rotterdam. I was a housekeeper, a gardener, a cook, a servant—any job that would keep me alive."

"The days stretched into weeks, weeks into months, and months into years. Time lost all meaning; each moment felt like an eternity—with each flicker of hope extinguished under the lash of a whip, a slap from the back of a hand, or a punch from a clenched fist. I longed for death—yet it would not come. Instead, I grew old and ugly."

"My looks had been my curse, attracting too much unwanted attention, but with age came a form of freedom. With it, I made my way to Boston, where I was employed as a housekeeper for Cunegonde's family. They were the first to treat me with kindness, and it was with them I finally found refuge."

A tear rolled down her cheek, the shadows of memory flickering to life, as she saw the barren walls of her prison cell in Azov, hearing the anguished cries of her fellow captives echoing into the gloom, feeling the bite of chains upon her wrists, the dull ache of bruises that would never fade.

"You asked how I endured," she said softly. "The truth is, there were times I did not. Times when all seemed lost, and darkness was all I knew." She gazed into space, watching the ghosts from her past dance while her tale spun. "It was in those moments that stories became my refuge. I would weave tales of hope and courage, of good triumphing over evil. And in the telling, I found the strength to go on. To believe there was still light to be found, even in the deepest of nights."

The Old Woman scanned the rolling waves; her milky eyes clouded with memory. "There were times I wished to die," she said softly. "When the darkness threatened to consume me, and hope seemed but a distant dream. But I found solace in the unlikeliest of places. Amidst the squalor and suffering, bonds were formed, and friendships forged, giving me strength when my own had failed."

She shook her head, a wry smile twisting her lips. "In bondage, we became each other's light in the darkness, sharing tales of home and hearth to chase away the shadows. Laughter echoed in that fetid place, and in each other's eyes, we found our humanity."

"Your courage is a testament to the resilience of the human spirit," Candide said.

"Despair is a choice, as is hope," she replied. "When all seemed lost, it was the stories we shared that lit the way forward. A reminder that there was still beauty to be found, even in the darkest of places. As long as we had each other, the light endured."

Silence fell over the group, her words resonating with each passenger. Candide gazed at the Old Woman with newfound respect, humbled by the depths of suffering she had endured. If anyone had cause to despair, it was her. Yet still, her spirit remained unbroken.

Candide squeezed the Old Woman's hand, his voice rough with emotion. "Your light has guided us from darkness," he said. "And your stories have given us hope, a most precious gift. You have my eternal gratitude, dear lady, for showing us the way."

The Old Woman's eyes gleamed, twin stars amidst the gathering dusk. "The light was always there, within each of you," she replied gently. "Sometimes, it just needs a spark to shine through."

A tender smile graced her lips as she gazed at each passenger in turn. "Together, there is no darkness we cannot overcome."

Her harrowing tale echoing deep within Candide's heart. How foolish he had been to blindly accept Pangloss's empty optimism in the face of such suffering. The Old Woman had endured evils beyond imagination yet emerged with her spirit unbroken. "Your story has opened my eyes," Candide said softly. "To persevere as you have, in the face of such adversity—it is a lesson I shall not soon forget."

Martin scoffed, his cynicism unmoved. "The only lesson is that this world of ours is cruel beyond measure. To survive it, one must have a heart of stone."

Cunegonde took the Old Woman's hand, her voice hushed with reverence. "You are the light that has guided us all. Your hope has given us strength, your stories have given us wings to rise above our sorrow."

"And together, we shall continue to rise," the Old Woman said quietly. "However long the night, the dawn will come." The Old Woman gazed out at the rippling sea. The boat's steady rocking, a soothing balm to her weary bones.

Candide settled down beside her. "Your story was heartbreaking, madam. I can scarcely imagine the horrors you have endured."

"The human spirit is resilient, young man. It endures far more than one might expect." Her gaze turned inward, shadows flickering through her memory. "Many times, I yearned for death. An end to the suffering. Yet, an inner flame persisted, unyielding to the darkness."

Martin grunted, crossing his arms. "Your tale confirms what I have long believed. This world of ours is cruel and unjust. There is no greater purpose to our suffering."

The Old Woman shook her head, turning to face the pessimist. "You are wrong, my dear Martin. Purpose can be found even in suffering, if one looks for the light amidst the darkness." Her voice grew quieter. "In my darkest hours, it was the bonds between my fellow captives that gave me strength. Their stories, woven from hope and longing, lit a candle to guide me through the long night."

Cunegonde reached out, clasping the Old Woman's gnarled hands. "Your courage humbles me, madam. I do not know if I could endure such hardships with your strength and grace."

A thoughtful silence fell over the group as the boat cut through the waves, bearing them ever closer to the shores of Cuba and an uncertain future. But for now, they had each other.

With half of her buttocks gone and only half of her cataracts removed, the Old Woman blinked against the glare of the morning sun, her eyes watering from the pain. But still, she smiled. After all she had endured, a little discomfort was nothing.

As the boat glided into the port of Havana, they gazed at the colorful buildings lining the harbor—a mosaic of pinks, blues, and yellows beneath a cloudless sky. Somewhere in this vibrant city, they hoped to find what they sought.

Cunegonde helped the Old Woman off the boat in Havana. She blinked in the bright sunlight. After the long dark night and the dim cabin lights, the world seemed dazzling and disorienting.

Martin emerged from the car rental, looking grim. "There's been a complication. I couldn't get us a rental car—they're requiring all sorts of paperwork and ID we don't have. Looks like we're on our own to find a clinic and a place to stay."

Candide shook his head, steadying the Old Woman as she wobbled on the walkway. "We knew this wouldn't be easy. But we'll figure something out. For now, let's just get to the city. Maybe we can find a taxi, or public transit."

They made their slow way out of the port terminal, the Old Woman clinging to Cunegonde's arm. Her eyes were still inflamed, her steps hesitant. Cunegonde's heart ached at the sight of her.

Outside of the terminal, an old Chevrolet was idling, a man leaning against the hood. He glanced up as they emerged, then strode over. "Welcome to Havana, I am Cacambo. Damas y caballeros, Could I be of service to you?"

Candide responded, "Maybe—Do you know an eye clinic where they can help our companion here? She has terrible pain and inflammation in her eyes after cataract surgery."

Cacambo smiled. "Sí, Señor. I know an eye clinic and staff who can properly treat this woman's eyes. Please get in."

Martin and Cunegonde exchanged a glance. It seemed too good to be true. But the Old Woman was flagging in the heat, her eyes growing more painful. Candide met Cacambo's gaze and nodded to Martin and Cunegonde.

"Thank you," Cunegonde said, her voice relieved. "You have no idea what this means to us."

"You are most welcome," Cacambo said. "Now come."

Candide slid into the backseat beside the Old Woman, who sighed in relief at being off her feet. As Cacambo steered them through the crowded streets, Candide studied him surreptitiously. He seemed kind enough, with a neat beard, a short crew cut, and an air of brisk competence. His sun-kissed skin was the color of well-worn leather. Though not tall, he had a reassuring solidity in his sturdy frame—a latent strength that spoke of resilience and survival.

But after their encounter with the Grand Inquisitor, Candide knew better than to take anything at face value. "How did you know we were coming?" Candide asked.

Cacambo's eyes crinkled at the corners. "I have a gift for finding those in need of help. And for helping them, of course."

"A gift," Candide said with a flat tone. His fist still ached from punching the Grand Inquisitor, a burst of violence he still couldn't quite believe. But he wouldn't hesitate to do the same to Cacambo if this turned out to be a trick.

Cacambo grinned, unconcerned with Candide's skepticism. "Here we are," he said, pulling up before a nondescript white building with a worn sign reading "Clínica Oftalmológica Dr. Fidel y Dr. Raúl" that hung crookedly above the entrance.

"Here is the eye clinic. If you'll help your companion inside, the staff will see to her immediately."

Candide tensed, clutching the Old Woman's arm. But one look at her exhausted, drawn face fortified his resolve. They had nowhere else to turn. "All right," he said. "But I'll be watching you closely, Cacambo."

"I would expect nothing less," Cacambo said. He came around to help Candide ease the Old Woman from the car. "I give you my word, she will be well cared for here. Please, come in."

Candide met Martin's gaze over the roof of the car, seeing his own wary hope reflected there. They had journeyed long and far, through dangers and despair and the deepest darkness of the human heart. But it seemed they had finally found a place of refuge. Pangloss could be right after all. He took a deep breath of the warm Cuban air and led the Old Woman into the clinic.

Chapter 10

We shall not carry out a revolutionary medicine with capitalist and bourgeois methods. Our people will not only know how to defend the revolution and defend the homeland. They will also know how to defend their health. ~ Fidel Castro

As the heavy door swung closed behind them, the vibrant buzz of Havana's streets was replaced by a hushed tranquility. White walls and the familiar, sterile scent of a medical facility enveloped them. Candide felt the tension in his shoulders ease slightly as he led the Old Woman into the clinic, with Cunegonde following close behind, trailed by Martin and Cacambo.

Candide glanced at Cunegonde, noting the worry creasing her brow. He gently squeezed the Old Woman's hand in reassurance before approaching the receptionist. Cacambo, standing at a respectful distance, gave them an encouraging nod.

"We're seeking medical assistance for our dear friend," Candide explained, indicating the Old Woman now resting on a nearby chair. "Her vision has been clouded since she had cataract surgery in her eyes a few days ago. Do you have skilled surgeons who can restore her sight?"

The receptionist nodded, as she checked the schedule. "Dr. Raúl should be available shortly. Please have a seat while you wait."

Candide sighed in relief, the tension in his shoulders loosening a bit more. Their luck seemed to be finally changing. Yet Martin's dour expression persisted. "Don't get your hopes up just yet," he cautioned in an undertone. "Revolutionary medicine, like revolution itself, has its limits. We'll see."

Candide bristled. Martin's skepticism was beginning to grate on him. "Then why did you bring us to Cuba in the first place?"

"Because that was the only boat I could get to get us out of Miami, it's not like I had time to consult my travel agent," Martin retorted.

While Cacambo stood by the door, Candide, Cunegonde, and Martin took their seats in the sparse but clean waiting area. A large Cuban flag and an imposing portrait of Fidel Castro hung on one wall, accompanied by a bold slogan: *¡Igualdad para todos en la luz y en la sombra!*

Candide's rudimentary Spanish allowed him to translate the phrase. "Equality for all, in light and in shadow," he mouthed deliberately, enunciating each syllable.

The sentiment resonated with Candide. If the revolutionary government aimed to provide healthcare equally to all citizens, regardless of status or wealth, then perhaps there was hope for the Old Woman.

Cunegonde nodded, also heartened by the slogan's promise. But Martin snorted with derision. "Equality is a fantasy peddled by despots and demagogues," he said under his breath. "Mark my words, this clinic will prove just as incompetent and corrupt as any other."

Candide bit his tongue. Debating Martin would be as fruitless as shouting at the tide. For now, he chose to cling to hope that the Old Woman would receive the eye care needed in this proletariat paradise. Furthermore, they had no other choice. A nurse entered and beckoned them into an examination room.

The nurse led them into a modest yet spotless examination room, gesturing for the Old Woman to sit on the table. Candide and Cunegonde flanked her on either side, lending their support. "The doctor will be with you shortly," the nurse informed them in accented but serviceable English. "Please complete these forms first."

She handed Candide a clipboard with medical forms, all in Spanish. He stared at it blankly, then turned his pleading eyes to Cacambo. Taking the paperwork from Candide, Cacambo quickly filled it out. Handing it back, he bid them all farewell.

"I must return to the docks now. Please let me know how the surgery goes. I wish your dear friend all the best!"

"Thank you, Cacambo." Candide's heart swelled with gratitude for their stalwart companion. Candide turned to grasp the Old Woman's gnarled hand. "Not long now," he said gently. "These fine doctors will have your eyes fixed up in no time, just wait and see!"

The Old Woman gave a tremulous smile. "I appreciate the optimism, my boy," she replied. "But these old eyes have endured much hardship. I scarcely dare to hope anymore."

Candide's heart ached at her words. How much suffering this poor soul had known! Now she was half-blind with only one buttock. If anyone deserved a reprieve, a taste of something better, it was her.

Candide squeezed the Older Woman's hand. She sighed heavily; her milky eyes downcast.

"Hope is a dangerous thing when you're my age," she murmured. "I've learned to expect little and appreciate what I have. But . . . " A shy smile teased her lips. "I'll admit, the thought of seeing again makes my heart flutter like a schoolgirl's. As for my missing buttock, I came to terms with it long ago."

Candide knelt before her, clasping her hands in his. "Have faith, dear friend! Today your darkness ends, and a new dawn begins!"

The Old Woman chuckled, patting his cheek. "My dear Candide, you are always an optimist. Well, I suppose a little hope can't hurt."

Martin sighed, shaking his head as they waited in the sterile examination room. "Hope is a fragile thing, my dear Candide. Best not to get carried away before we know what these Cuban doctors can actually do."

Cunegonde shot Martin a reproachful look. "Must you always expect the worst?" she chided.

Martin held up his hands. "Merely cautioning against false hope, my lady."

The door opened, and a doctor entered. "¡Hola, amigos!" He greeted them with a warm smile. "I am Dr. Raúl. Now, who is the patient needing my revolutionary cure?" His hair, black as the richest soil of Pinar del Río, was cropped close to his head. A sparse goatee outlined his strong chin, his white coat stark against his tanned skin.

Candide replied, "This is our dear friend, in dire need of your medical expertise . . . " Clasping Cunégonde's hand firmly, the Old Woman allowed herself to be led to the examination chair. The doctor nodded, his expression growing serious as he examined the Old Woman's eyes.

"I see . . . half a cataract in both eyes," he murmured. "But do not worry, comrade. Our revolutionary medicine shall restore your vision!"

Dr. Raúl outlined the planned procedure, expressing his admiration for the cataract surgery techniques developed in America under the DEI guidelines. He noted that in Cuba's workers' paradise, all patients received equal treatment.

"No one is more special than others," he declared. "So, we shall remove all cataracts completely for every patient!"

Candide beamed, gripping the Old Woman's hands excitedly. "You hear that? These skilled revolutionaries will return your sight! Is that not wondrous news?" The Old Woman nodded, scarcely daring to hope. Martin eyed the doctor with skepticism but held his tongue.

Cunegonde smiled, encouraged. "Have faith, my dear faithful servant. Your trials will soon be at an end."

Dr. Fidel strode into the examination room, having finished his last surgery of the day. The Old Woman's heart leapt as the famous revolutionary doctor approached her. His eyes were piercing blue reminiscent of the Caribbean Sea on a cloudless day. A robust man of medium height, his belly bore testament to his love for a good Cuban feast, yet his movements were graceful and purposeful, like those of a seasoned salsa dancer.

"Let's have a look, shall we?" Dr. Fidel said, leaning in to examine her eyes. The Old Woman held her breath, scarcely daring to move. After a moment, Dr. Fidel straightened up, stroking his bushy beard, and nodded at Dr. Raúl. "Yes, I agree with your assessment, comrade brother. We can certainly restore this patient's vision with our exemplary Cuban techniques!"

Candide clasped his hands, his face alight. "Oh, praise be! You will give our dear friend back her sight?"

"Of course!" Dr. Fidel declared. "Simply sign these release forms, and we will begin immediately. In the name of the revolution, we shall bring forth the light!"

Martin frowned, skeptical of the bombastic doctors. But the Old Woman silenced him with a smile before he could find fault. She would not let cynicism ruin this moment. The Old Woman took the pen, and with a flourish, signed the forms. No matter what happened, she had faith in the power of revolutionary medicine. Her trials were at an end.

Cunegonde stepped forward, her voice tinged with concern. "When would you do the operation, doctors?"

Dr. Raúl and Dr. Fidel exchanged a look and nodded. "At once, señorita!" they proclaimed in unison. "There is no time to waste when it comes to restoring the eyesight of our fellow proletarian!" Their zeal took Cunegonde aback. She glanced uncertainly at the Old Woman, who sat very still in her chair.

"Right away? But shouldn't we let her rest first?" Cunegonde asked.

Dr. Fidel waved a hand. "No need, no need! We shall whisk her into surgery now and return her good as new in no time." He clapped the Old Woman on the shoulder. "What do you say, comrade sister? Are you ready to embrace the gift of sight?"

The Old Woman took a deep breath. "Yes," she said with conviction, "I am ready."

Dr. Raúl gestured to the nurses. "Excellent! Prep the patient at once. We make revolutionary history today!"

As the staff bustled around her, the Old Woman felt Cunegonde squeeze her hand. "Be strong, dear friend," Cunegonde whispered. "Your suffering will soon be over."

Amidst a flurry of commotion, the Old Woman was whisked away to undergo the promised procedure. Her rickety wheelchair vanished through the swinging doors, while Candide, Cunegonde, and Martin watched with anticipation.

Too anxious to sit, Candide began pacing the small waiting room, his footsteps echoing off the sterile white walls. Cunegonde sat primly in one of the stiff chairs, her hands folded neatly in her lap, but her fingers fidgeted with a loose thread on her skirt. Martin slouched in the corner, appearing half asleep, but his eyes followed Candide's restless movements.

"Do you think they can really restore her sight?" Candide asked, pausing his pacing for a moment.

Martin shrugged. "Who's to say? The doctors spoke boldly enough. But words are cheap."

"We must have faith," Cunegonde insisted with a gentle tone, though she sounded less than fully convinced.

The hours crawled by at a torturous pace. The trio exchanged few words, each lost in their own thoughts as they waited.

Finally, after what seemed like an eternity, the doors swung open. Dr. Fidel emerged; his surgical mask pulled down to reveal a triumphant smile, Dr. Raúl following closely behind. "The operation was a success!" he declared. "Your dear friend will see again thanks to the miracle of Cuban medicine! All of the cataracts were removed, as promised."

Candide hesitated, almost afraid to believe it could be true. "Her vision . . . it's really restored?"

Dr. Fidel clapped him on the back. "As good as new, comrade! Now we celebrate!"

Cunegonde's eyes widened in disbelief. "¡Milagro!" she exclaimed, "Is it really possible? Can her sight truly be restored?"

Despite his earlier doubts, even Martin displayed cautious optimism upon hearing the news. "Well, I'll be," he murmured. "Maybe there is something to this revolutionary medicine."

Candide was nearly jumping for joy. "I knew it! I knew our faith would be rewarded!" He grasped Dr. Fidel's hands with enthusiasm. "When can we see her?"

"Right away, my friends!" Dr. Fidel declared as he led them down the hall to the recovery room. The Old Woman was sitting up in bed, a large white bandage over her eyes. As they entered, she turned toward them with an expectant look on her face.

"The time has come to reveal the fruits of our labor," Dr. Fidel announced. With a dramatic flourish, he unwound the gauze wrapped around the Old Woman's head. The trio waited with anticipation as she slowly opened her eyes. The Old Woman blinked several times and squinted at them in confusion.

"Well? Can you see us?" Candide asked with hope in his voice.

The Old Woman tilted her head, staring in Candide's direction. "I see . . . something," she said with hesitation. "But it's quite fuzzy . . . . "

Cunegonde clasped her hands to her chest. "But you can make us out? Your vision is restored?"

"I'm not sure . . . " the Old Woman trailed off, blinking hard. "You, there, in the purple coat. Are you Cunegonde or Candide?" The trio exchanged dismayed glances. The miracle of Cuban medicine had its limits. Candide's face fell, but he tried to hide his disappointment. "It's me, Candide. Don't worry, I'm sure your vision will continue to improve."

He turned to Dr. Fidel with forced optimism. "This is still a vast improvement, is it not? Before, she could see nothing at all!"

Dr. Fidel cleared his throat, looking uncomfortable. "Yes, well . . . it may take some time for the full effects to emerge. We must be patient."

Martin had been silent up until now, his arms folded over his chest as he observed the scene with suspicion. Finally, he spoke up. "I'm an eye doctor, but it seems to me her vision hasn't improved one bit," he remarked with sarcasm. "Perhaps your revolutionary techniques aren't as miraculous as you claim."

Dr. Fidel bristled at the criticism. "Nonsense! The procedure was a complete success. Her eyes merely need time to adjust, that's all."

"Adjust to what?" Martin shot back. "Seeing fuzzy shapes and colors? I fear you've promised more than you could deliver, my friend."

Candide glanced between them anxiously. "Please, let's not argue. I still have faith this will all work out."

But Martin was not easily mollified. He leaned in close to examine the Old Woman's eyes himself, shaking his head with a skeptical sigh. "I'll believe it when I see it," he muttered. "And so far, I'm not seeing any miracles."

The Old Woman continued blinking slowly, still not completely awake from the anesthesia. As the room came into better focus, fuzzy shapes and colors began to emerge. She squinted, trying to make sense of the hazy images dancing before her.

"¿Qué es esto?" she murmured. "No puedo ver claramente." The anesthesia was making her speak in Spanish.

Candide leaned in; concern etched on his face. "What do you see, my dear?" The Old Woman pointed a trembling finger. "Eso . . . ¿es un gato o un cactus?"

Martin, suppressing a snicker, "She's seeing cats as cacti! At least, her Spanish is flawless."

A wobbly shape sat on the counter, indistinguishable to her recovering eyes. Candide's shoulders slumped as the Old Woman could not tell a simple cat from a cactus. The surgery had clearly failed.

Martin clicked his tongue, vindicated. "Just as I suspected. Her vision is no better, perhaps even worse." He shot an accusatory look at Dr. Fidel. "Some revolutionary medicine this turned out to be."

Dr. Fidel held up his hands defensively. "I assure you, with time, her eyes will adjust. We must have patience!"

But Candide was crestfallen, their last glimmer of hope extinguished. "It seems patience is not enough. Your promised miracle has failed us, Doctor."

The Old Woman squinted hard at the fuzzy shapes. "Everything is a blur. I cannot distinguish anything clearly."

Candide shook his head in disappointment. After all their trials and tribulations, fate was still not on their side. "What devilry is this?" he cried out in anguish. "Has the surgery truly failed? Could our dear Old Woman be doomed to a life of darkness?"

Having remained silent up to now, Dr. Raúl held up a hand in reassurance. "Calm yourself, my friend. The fault is mine, not fate's." He sighed, a look of remorse on his face. "You see, there was a . . . slight miscalculation on my part."

"A miscalculation?" Candide, incredulous.

"Yes, a small but critical error," Dr. Raúl admitted. "In my haste, I confess that I mistook the scalpel for the suture."

"You *what?!*" Candide exclaimed.

"As a result, the incisions were not as . . . precisely made as they could have been," the doctor continued sheepishly. "Her vision may be, shall we say, a tad unconventional for some time."

Candide buried his face in his hands. After coming all this way, after placing all their hopes on the promise of Cuban medicine, the journey had ended in utter failure.

"Unconventional?" Candide muttered through his fingers; his voice laced with bitterness. "She sees cats as cacti, for heaven's sake!"

Dr. Raúl opened his mouth as if to defend himself further but thought better of it. The Old Woman's repeated murmurs of "¿Gato o cactus?" punctuated the momentary silence, as she squinted at the blurry shape before her.

"Unconventional is certainly one way to put it," Martin remarked in a snarky voice. "Seeing felines as desert flora seems unconventional indeed."

Candide gave him an irritated glare. Martin shrugged with open hands. "I did warn you hope can be a fickle thing, my friend," he added, his tone carrying a hint of *I told you so.*

Before Candide could respond, the examination room door burst open with a resounding crash. Cacambo came tumbling through, eyes wide with alarm. "Señor Candide!" he cried. "You must flee at once! The police—they are coming for you!"

Candide's anger evaporated, giving way to shock and confusion. "The police? What are you talking about?"

Cacambo frantically explained how the police officers from the K9 unit had intercepted him at the port. They had shown him a photograph of Candide, declaring him wanted for murder in the United States. Even now, they were rapidly approaching the clinic, accompanied by a pack of snarling police dogs.

Candide went pale. To have come so far, only to be captured now? It was a nightmare. He exchanged an urgent look with Cunegonde and Martin.

"Come with me, quickly!" Cacambo urged.

"Go now, my love," Cunegonde pleaded, tearing streaming down her cheeks.

Martin piped in, "Make haste, my dear Candide. In your absence, I shall take care of Cunegonde and the Old Woman."

After a quick hug and a kiss with Cunegonde. Candide left with Cacambo. The pair fled through the back corridors of the clinic, the barking and shouting of the police officers echoed behind them. Candide's heart pounded as he ran. They burst through a side door into a narrow alleyway. The sunlight momentarily blinded Candide as his eyes adjusted from the dim light of the clinic. In the near distance, the wail of police sirens mingled with the lively sounds of Old Havana.

"This way!" Cacambo shouted, beckoning Candide down the alley. Their footsteps pounded on the worn cobblestones. Candide glanced back, half-expecting to see the police rounding the corner behind them. For now, however, the alley remained eerily empty. Cacambo led him on a twisting, zigzagging route through Havana's backstreets. They raced past weathered colonial buildings and crumbling piles of bricks, with occasional passersby gaping in surprise.

At last, Cacambo brought them skidding to a halt beside a battered blue Lada. "Get in!" he urged, wrenching open the passenger door. Candide crammed himself into the back seat while Cacambo jumped into the driver's seat. With a sputter and a roar, the old car jolted forward, carrying them away just as the first police cars came screeching around the corner.

Candide's pounding heart began to ease as Cacambo steered them expertly through Havana's chaotic streets distancing themselves from the police. They had made it. For now, at least, they were free.

Chapter 11

*Of all religions, the Christian should of course in-
spire the most tolerance, but until now Christians
have been the most intolerant of all men. ~ Voltaire*

The fetid stench of diesel and brine filled Candide's nostrils as he
huddled in the dark, cramped hold of the cargo ship. The thrum of
the engines vibrated through the cold metal floor. Cacambo's steady
snoring beside him was the only buffer keeping his panic at bay.

In Havana, they had slipped aboard in the dead of night, the
captain, Cacambo's cousin, smuggling them below decks among
the shipping containers. He had pressed a finger to his lips, his eyes
twinkling with mischief as he ushered them into their hiding spot.
"No one will find you here, amigos. Safe passage to Paraguay!"

Now Candide shifted, trying to stretch his aching muscles
without making a sound. *How long have they been at sea?* It felt
like an eternity since he'd seen the sun. His stomach rumbled, the
meager scraps of food Cacambo had scavenged barely taking the

edge off his hunger. He thought of Cunegonde and wondered if she had made it safely away. A pang of longing pierced his heart—*would he ever gaze upon her face again?*

Cacambo's eyes fluttered open, meeting Candide's worried stare. "We'll be alright, my friend," he whispered. "Soon we'll be in my homeland."

Candide managed a weak smile, drawing courage from Cacambo's calm demeanor. His resourcefulness and local connections had gotten him this far. By helping Candide escape, Cacambo had become an accessory-after-the-fact. Candide owed him his life.

The engines slowed and the ship lurched as it came into port. Holding their breath, they waited for the telltale footsteps of the crew to pass. Soon they would be on solid ground again, fugitives in a foreign land with uncertain futures. Yet, Candide had put his trust in Cacambo.

Candide blinked and shaded his eyes with his hand as they adjusted to the bright Paraguayan sun. After days cramped in the dark hull of the ship, the light was nearly blinding. Cacambo led him quickly through the bustling port of Encarnación, keeping their heads down. Sticking to the shadows as much as possible, Cacambo guided Candide with ease through the maze of alleys and side streets.

They arrived at a modest adobe building on the outskirts of town. Cacambo knocked in a peculiar pattern and a tiny slot opened. After a rapid exchange in Guaraní, the door swung open. An elderly woman embraced Cacambo, weeping with joy. "My son, you've come home!"

Cacambo introduced Candide to his mother, explaining their predicament—Candide was wanted for murder, and he had become an accessory by helping Candide evade the police in Cuba. She ushered them inside, insisting they eat and rest. They would hide out here for the time being.

Candide was penniless. He lay on a straw mat in the corner of Cacambo's childhood room, trying to process the whirlwind of events that had flung him across the world. Here, in this still room, memories of his past life crept up on him like specters at dusk. He could recall Dr. Pangloss's lectures—each a labyrinth of logic and philosophy—eloquent arguments espousing the belief that this was the best of all possible worlds.

A few days passed, and Candide's restlessness grew. He could not live on Cacambo's charity forever. He decided to look for work as a doctor at a Jesuit hospital nearby.

The next day, Cacambo returned with good news. "I've arranged an interview for you at the hospital," he told Candide. "My cousin works for the administrator there."

Candide felt a swell of gratitude. Once again, Cacambo had come through for him. The following morning, Candide donned his finest attire, striving to appear professional. Despite feeling overwhelmed, he knew this opportunity was his best chance to stay under the radar, earn a living, and save enough money to eventually reunite with Cunegonde. Taking a deep breath, he followed Cacambo to the hospital. As he sat nervously in the administrator's office, fidgeting with the brim of his hat, he prayed that the administrator would give him a chance.

The administrator, a portly man dressed in a long black cassock, with a meticulously groomed mustache, regarded him with a cool demeanor sitting behind a large mahogany desk. "So, Candide, tell me why you're interested in joining our esteemed hospital?" he asked.

Candide cleared his throat. "Oh well, sir, I've always had a passion for helping people, especially when it comes to their vision. I believe that every person, regardless of their station in life, deserves access to quality eye care."

The administrator chuckled. "Admirable sentiments, Candide, truly." His tone held a note of amusement. "But tell me, have you ever worked in a charity hospital setting before?"

"Well, no," Candide admitted. "But I'm a quick learner and very dedicated. I spent a year studying ophthalmology and assisting professors at my university. I would be honored to use my skills to serve your patients."

The administrator raised an eyebrow. "Is that so? We shall see, Candide. The life of a physician requires more than book learning. If you wish to join our team, you must prove yourself capable."

Candide nodded with enthusiasm. "I understand, sir. I'm ready to do whatever it takes."

The administrator studied him a moment longer, then nodded. "Very well. I will give you a chance, Candide. Do not disappoint me."

Candide exhaled in relief. This was his opportunity to start a new life here. He would not squander it. "Thank you, sir. I promise you won't regret this."

The administrator handed him some forms. "Fill these out. Report here first thing tomorrow to begin your duties. And Candide—" he fixed him with a serious look "—welcome to the team."

Candide took the forms with slightly trembling hands, his excitement evident. This was his chance to put his skills to use and make a difference. As he began filling out the paperwork, the administrator regarded him with a keen eye. "You seem quite eager, Candide. Tell me, what do you hope to gain from joining us here?"

Candide glanced up. "Well, sir, I hope to help people, of course. To make a positive impact through medicine."

The administrator nodded. "Commendable. But you should know, we cater to a very specific clientele here."

Candide furrowed his brow in confusion. "I'm not sure I understand, sir."

"Let's just say we provide care on a priority basis," the administrator continued cryptically. "Your duties may require a certain . . . pragmatism."

Candide hesitated. "I see. Well, I'm sure I can adapt, sir."

"Good. That kind of flexibility will serve you well here." The administrator smiled, but the expression didn't reach his eyes.

Candide signed the last form with a flourish and handed the stack back to the administrator.

"Excellent. We'll have someone show you around shortly," the man said, gathering up the papers. "But first, a bit of advice." He leaned forward, steepling his fingers under his chin. "Our patrons here expect the highest quality care. But resources being what they are, we must . . . prioritize. I trust you understand?"

Candide shifted in his seat. "I believe I do, sir."

"Good. Not everyone can stomach our approach. But those who adapt tend to thrive." The administrator stood, signaling the end of the meeting. As Candide rose to shake his hand, a glint of satisfaction in the man's eyes made him uneasy.

"Thank you for this opportunity, sir," Candide said politely. "I look forward to getting started."

"As do I, my boy. As do I." The administrator clapped him on the back.

Candide forced a smile, tamping down his misgivings. He reminded himself he was here to help people, however he could. *After all, how bad could it be?* He followed the aide down the plush-carpeted hallway, glancing around at the lavish furnishings and ornate decorations adorning the hospital. Crystal chandeliers, marble floors, gilded picture frames. It was quite different from the humble clinics where he had worked in Haiti. As they passed the waiting room, Candide noted the patients flipping through magazines and sipping complimentary cappuccinos. Staff in crisp uniforms hovered nearby, attending politely to any need or request.

"Impressive, isn't it?" the aide remarked, noticing Candide's wandering gaze. "We aim to provide five-star service here."

Candide gave an absent nod. His earlier conversation with the administrator echoed in his mind.

Soon after starting at the Jesuit hospital, Candide worked with unwavering diligence and was an exemplary employee. Though troubled by the administrator's directives to prioritize the wealthy over the poor, Candide did his best to provide care to all patients.

After long days at the hospital, Candide would return home exhausted yet satisfied at having helped those in need. There, his loyal friend Cacambo kept their humble house in order and had found odd jobs here and there to supplement Candide's modest income from the hospital.

"We may not live in luxury, my friend, but we have a roof over our heads and food on the table," Cacambo said cheerfully one evening as they ate a simple meal.

Although fatigued, Candide smiled. "You're right, Cacambo. And we're slowly but surely saving money to reunite with Cunegonde, the Old Woman, and Martin one day."

Cacambo nodded. "Have faith, Candide. Our fortunes may be modest at the moment, but so long as we have our health and each other, we have all we need."

Candide retired to bed that night with Cacambo's words lingering in his thoughts. Though their future remained uncertain, the loyalty and optimism of his steadfast friend gave him hope. Each day brought new challenges to the hospital, but Candide drew strength from knowing he and Cacambo were united by their principles. No matter what happened, they would face it together.

The next morning, Candide headed to the hospital with renewed vigor, determined to provide the best care possible to all patients, rich or poor. Upon arriving, however, he was promptly summoned to the administrator's office.

"Candide, I must discuss a matter of some concern," the administrator said in a grave voice. "It has come to my attention that you have been treating the indigenous poor who come to our hospital."

Candide shifted in his seat. "With respect sir, as a doctor it is my duty to care for all patients equally, regardless of background or means. Aren't we all God's children?"

The administrator laughed. "Ah, Candide, your naiveté is as charming as it is impractical. I must remind you that while all are indeed God's children, our resources are more divinely bestowed upon those whose pocketbooks have been similarly graced."

"But sir," Candide protested, "didn't you say this was a charity hospital when you hired me?"

"A figure of speech, my naive friend," the administrator chuckled. "We must prioritize those who fund our work. The peasants can seek care elsewhere."

That evening at home, Candide described what he had observed to a sympathetic Cacambo. "This is not the medicine I believe in," Candide lamented.

"Do not lose heart, my friend," Cacambo said. "We must find a way to help the poor, with or without the hospital's approval."

Candide agreed, "Thank you for the suggestion. That is what my mentor, Jake Anabaptiste, would do."

Cacambo puzzled, "Jake who?"

"Let me tell you about him . . . "

From then on, Candide and Cacambo secretly ventured into remote villages whenever they could, bringing medical aid to the indigenous poor. Over the centuries, the indigenous people had been converted by the Jesuits but had also lost their lands. As their faith grew stronger, their poverty deepened.

A month later, Candide was summoned again to the administrator's office. He entered tentatively, unsure of what to expect.

Seated behind a large mahogany desk, the administrator peered at Candide over his spectacles. "Candide, my boy," he began in a smooth tone, "I've been hearing excellent reports about your work in the remote villages. You've made quite an impression."

Candide flushed with pride. "Thank you, sir. I'm just trying my best to help those in need."

"And admirably so," said the administrator. He leaned forward, fixing Candide with an intent look. "In fact, I believe you're ready for more . . . responsibility."

Candide's eyes widened. "Responsibility, sir?"

"Yes. You've proven yourself more than capable out there, which is why I've decided to promote you."

"Promote me?" Candide could not believe his ears.

"That's right. You shall now oversee all medical missions to the remotest villages. Consider it a testament to your dedication and skills." The administrator said, smiling with practiced benevolence.

Candide was speechless for a moment. Then he found his voice again. "Thank you, sir! I'm honored by your faith in me. I won't let you down."

The administrator chuckled. "Oh, I have no doubt, my boy. For your first mission, I direct you to the Oreillon village, the most remote village from the hospital. No one has ever successfully reached that village and returned. Now run along—and remember, with greater responsibility comes greater . . . discretion."

Candide nodded with enthusiasm before taking his leave, nearly bursting with pride. As he walked back to the clinic, he began making mental lists of all he hoped to accomplish in his new position. Brimming with optimism about his new role, he entered the clinic and was greeted by his trusted friend and companion, Cacambo.

"Candide, you look so cheerful. What news are you bringing?" asked Cacambo.

"Wonderful news, my friend! The administrator has promoted me to head all medical missions to the remotest villages. Isn't it marvelous?" exclaimed Candide.

Cacambo's face fell slightly. "The remotest villages? But some of those places can be quite . . . perilous."

Candide waved away his concerns. "Nonsense, dear Cacambo! With this promotion, I'll finally be able to truly make a difference for those most in need."

Cacambo nodded. "Of course, I'm happy for you, my friend."

"Oh, and the administrator made it quite clear I'll need to exercise discretion in my new role," Candide continued. "But helping people is worth any risk, wouldn't you agree?"

Cacambo gave a weak smile. "You know I'm always by your side, Candide."

Candide clapped Cacambo on the back. "Fret not, trusty Cacambo! Together, we shall bring health and hope to even the most remote corners of this land. Now come, we must start planning our first mission, to the Oreillon village!"

One week later, early morning at the Jesuit hospital, Candide strode with purpose and determination down the hall, Cacambo trailing behind. Though Candide exuded confidence, Cacambo noticed the tension in his shoulders. Stepping into the courtyard, Candide paused, taking a deep breath. The lush gardens reminded him of his childhood home—a simpler time before he got caught up in the administrator's web.

"Well, Cacambo, our work begins," Candide said, a bit wistfully.

"We'll help who we can, as best we're able," Cacambo assured him. "But we must be wise as serpents and gentle as doves."

Candide nodded. "You're right, of course. Still, I wish—"

"Candide!" A gruff voice interrupted. Manuel, the hospital's caretaker and mechanic strode over. "The jeep is ready, and all the medical supplies are loaded for your trip."

"Thank you, Manuel," said Candide.

"Be careful out there," Manuel warned. "The jungle is unforgiving, and the villages have their own rules."

"We will. And Manuel, please look after things while I'm gone."

"I'll do my best. Godspeed."

Candide gave Manuel a firm handshake and headed for the idling jeep. Cacambo gave Manuel a nod before following.

As Candide put the jeep in drive, he felt the weight of his mission. Beside him sat Cacambo, his steadfast companion. With optimism swelling in his heart, Candide drove onward into the looming jungle, towards the villages in need.

Chapter 12

You must have the Devil in you to succeed in any of the arts. ~ Voltaire

The bright fluorescent lights of the crowded waiting room stung Cunegonde's eyes as she sat next to the Old Woman. Around them, other seniors were flipping through outdated magazines or staring blankly ahead. The air was thick and humid, as the ceiling fan traced lazy circles overhead. Cunegonde suppressed a shudder, thinking back to their detention in Cuba. She could still hear the Old Woman's panicked cries when the police grabbed her frail arms. It had been weeks since they left Havana, and they hadn't heard from Candide.

"Don't worry, we're safe now," Cunegonde murmured, patting the Old Woman's hand.

The Old Woman squinted at the paperwork in her lap. "Thanks to Martin. Otherwise, we would still be locked up in Havana."

After Candide and Cacambo escaped, Cunegonde, Martin and the Old Woman were arrested by the Cuban police, who were alerted by Interpol that Candide was a fugitive wanted in the United States. Martin contacted his marine buddy, a judge advocate general, General Courtney Marshall Esq., stationed at the US embassy in Havana. Thanks to Martin's distinguished military service records, she was able to convince both US and Cuban authorities to drop all charges against the trio. Shortly after being released, they returned to Miami. Cunegonde and the Old Woman moved back to their condo in Key Biscayne. Martin found work as an ophthalmologist at a local VA clinic.

"Shh," Cunegonde said, "we are safe now." Ever since the disastrous eye surgery, the Old Woman's vision had gotten worse. Cunegonde knew they couldn't risk returning to the World's Best Eye Institute. Not after the way they'd left. A nurse called the Old Woman's name and Cunegonde helped her to her feet. As they shuffled down the hall, Cunegonde worried about how they would pay for this visit, but then she remembered the Old Woman had turned 65 a week ago. "Don't worry about money," Cunegonde said as they entered the exam room. "You qualify for Medicare now. We'll get you signed up."

The Old Woman looked uncertain. "Medicare? I don't know . . ."

"It will be fine," Cunegonde reassured her.

The doctor confirmed the Old Woman's vision was deteriorating rapidly. Instead of improving her vision, the cataract surgery had made her eyes worse, leaving her with poorer eyesight than before. She had glaucoma and her eyes remained severely inflamed. She needed specialized treatment, but without insurance the cost would be astronomical.

As they left the office, Cunegonde tried to remain upbeat. "Don't worry, we'll get you signed up for Medicare as soon as we get home. I'll make some calls."

Back at the condo, Cunegonde got to work. Medicare was a maze of red tape, and she decided to consult Milo Vanderdendur, the local health insurance salesman, who had an office in Key Biscayne.

Milo Vanderdendur arrived at the condo punctually, his briefcase in hand and a professional smile plastered on his face. His hair was a miraculous sculpture—a gravity-defying wave of glistening silver. His smile contained so many teeth that Cunegonde wondered if he were part shark. He wore a suit of intense cerulean blue.

Cunegonde greeted Milo with a smile. "Thank you for coming," leading Milo to a small sitting area where the Old Woman awaited.

As he flicked open his bulging briefcase, pamphlets and documents spilled across the glass coffee table. The Old Woman squinted at the paperwork strewn about, her expression one of rising apprehension, while Cunegonde sat beside her.

Milo Vanderdendur began his usual pitch with, "Greetings, esteemed residents of this palatial Key Biscayne condo! I come bearing tidings of healthcare marvels, for the venerable Old Woman has reached the illustrious age of 65 and must now navigate the labyrinthine realm of Medicare."

Cunegonde responded with relief, "Oh, how delightful of you to grace us with your presence, Milo Vanderdendur! Pray, enlighten us on the options available to our beloved Old Woman."

With enthusiasm, Milo continued, "Fear not, fair Cunegonde and beloved Old Woman, for I am here to guide you through the treacherous waters of healthcare choices. Behold, the traditional Medicare Plan, a venerable institution as old as time itself, offering Parts A and B with all the charm of a dusty tome in a forgotten library."

The Old Woman sighed. "Hmm, sounds rather antiquated."

"Ah, but fear not, dear Old Woman," Milo said. "I bring news of a brighter path! Feast your eyes upon the Medicare Advantage plans, a veritable treasure trove of medical delights! Part A, Part B, plus prescription drug coverage, and a plethora of additional perks await you, like a buffet of healthcare abundance!"

"Intriguing indeed!" Cunegonde spoke up. "But tell me, Milo, what sets these Advantage plans apart from the traditional Medicare?"

"Ah, my dear Cunegonde, the differences are as stark as night and day! The traditional Medicare Plan may offer a modicum of freedom, but it pales in comparison to the majesty of Advantage plans. Picture a grand ball where every step is a graceful dance, featuring low copayments and no deductibles, with the insurance company as your noble dance partner!" Milo gushed, pleased with his own imagery.

The Old Woman queried, "But what of the costs, Milo?"

"Ah, costs! A trifling matter, my dear Old Woman, when compared to the bountiful benefits of the Advantage plans. Why worry about coins when you can bask in the warm glow of comprehensive coverage and shiny pamphlets?"

Cunegonde interrupted the erudite salesman. "Pardon us, Milo Vanderdendur, but we find ourselves perplexed. How can these Advantage plans possibly outshine the traditional Medicare?"

Milo had his answer ready. "Ah, my dear Cunegonde, I understand your skepticism. But worry not, for I am here to shed light on the matter. Picture, if you will, a world where deductibles vanish like magic and copayments are as rare as a unicorn sighting."

"But surely there must be a catch, Milo," the Old Woman said with suspicion. "Nothing in this world comes without a price."

"Oh, you're quite right, dear Old Woman. But fear not, for the catch is but a trifle compared to the bountiful benefits bestowed upon you. Think of it as a tiny mouse in a vast field of cheese—hardly worth catching!"

"Pray tell, Milo, what exactly is this catch you speak of?" Cunegonde interjected.

"Very well," Milo answered, "while Advantage plans may offer lower out-of-pocket costs and additional perks, they also come with limitations on healthcare providers and networks. It's like having a golden cage—luxurious, yes, but with bars nonetheless."

"Aha!" Cunegonde responded. "We knew there had to be a catch. But do go on, Milo. What else should we be wary of?"

Milo Vanderdendur continued, his words well-rehearsed from years of experience. "Well, there's also the matter of prior authorizations and referrals for certain services, and the possibility of plan changes each year. But worry not, for with my expert guidance, you'll navigate these treacherous waters with ease!"

"Hmm," muttered the Old Woman, "it sounds like navigating a maze with blindfolds on."

"Oh, but think of the adventure, dear Old Woman! The thrill of the unknown, the excitement of discovery . . . like an odyssey through the land of healthcare!"

Next, Cunegonde asked, "Milo Vanderdendur, what about drug coverage? How does it compare to the traditional plan?"

"Ah, drug coverage, a topic as complex as unraveling a knitted sweater made by a blindfolded octopus—using all eight tentacles! Fear not, fair Cunegonde, for I shall endeavor to explain it in terms even a parrot could understand."

The Old Woman was becoming weary and impatient. "Please! Milo, spare us your aquatic and avian metaphors and get to the point."

To which Milo responded, "Of course, dear Old Woman. With the Advantage plans, drug coverage is often included, like a cherry on top of a sundae or an extra sprinkle of fairy dust. It's all part of the magical package compared to the traditional plan, a stalwart war horse in the battle of healthcare. While it does offer drug coverage under Part D, it's like a stubborn mule compared to the sleek racehorse of Advantage plans. There may be more hoops to jump through and coins to toss into the wishing well, but rest assured, the medication shall find its way into your hands eventually."

The Old Woman, hoping to cut through Milo's verbiage, asked, "So, with the Advantage plans, we're essentially getting all the drugs we need without the hassle?"

"Precisely, dear Old Woman!" Milo explained. "It's like having a genie in a bottle, ready to grant your every prescription wish with a mere flick of the wrist. And with my guidance, you'll be sipping from the fountain of pharmaceutical abundance in no time!"

Cunegonde, also weary and frowning, decided to pin Milo down as best she could. "Milo Vanderdendur, we have a rather curious inquiry for you. If you were to choose a Medicare plan for your own dear mother, which would it be: the Advantage plan or the traditional plan?"

As expected, Milo had a prepared answer. "Ah, what an intriguing hypothetical question, my dear Cunegonde! It's like asking whether one prefers a stroll through a rose garden or a swim in a pool filled with golden coins."

The Old Woman was ready to scream but composed herself and spoke with respect. "Please, Milo, enough with the flowery metaphors. We seek a straightforward answer."

Milo answered immediately. "I would undoubtedly opt for the Advantage plan. Why, you ask? Because it offers the best of both worlds—comprehensive coverage and a smorgasbord of extra perks, like a buffet of healthcare delights!"

Cunegonde had been weighing the advantages in her head, and hoping for more clarification, she pressed Milo further. "But what about the potential drawbacks? Surely you wouldn't want your mother to be caught in the snare of prior authorizations and network limitations."

With a flourish of hand gestures, Milo went on. "Do not underestimate the power of my expert guidance, fair Cunegonde! With my help, my mother would glide through the healthcare maze with the grace of a swan on a moonlit pond. Besides, who wouldn't want their dear old mom to enjoy the luxury of gym memberships and dental coverage?"

The Old Woman thought this over before answering, "I'm not sure about joining the gym. I have only one buttock. But I suppose there is some merit to your argument, Milo. However, what if your mother prefers the freedom to see any doctor without restriction?"

"An excellent point but fear not, for with the Advantage plan, my mother would have access to a wide network of doctors and specialists, like a bouquet of flowers in a vast garden. And if she ever desired a change of scent, well, that's what annual enrollment periods are for!"

Cunegonde sought resolution on the subject. "Your salesmanship is truly unparalleled, Milo. We will consider your advice carefully as we decide on the Old Woman's Medicare plan."

Feeling he had offered an excellent presentation on the pros and cons of Medicare plans, Milo thought he may as well wrap up the conversation. "I am humbled by your praise, fair Cunegonde. Should you require further guidance or wish to embark on the grand adventure of Medicare Advantage, you need only call upon me. Until then, adieu!"

"Farewell, Milo," the Old Woman said with some relief, "and may your mother's Medicare journey be as smooth as silk, whichever path she chooses."

A few days later, Cunegonde called Milo Vanderdendur. His phone rang only once before she was greeted with upbeat professionalism. "Hello, you've reached Milo's Health Insurance Emporium, where your health is our wealth! How may I assist you today?"

"Hi, Milo," Cunegonde said. "We have made our final decision on the Medicare options. We shall heed your counsel and embrace the Advantage plans with open arms!"

On the other end of the line, Milo pumped his fist in victory. "Splendid news! You won't regret this choice, I assure you. Why, with the comprehensive coverage and bountiful perks, it will be like having a personal concierge to cater to the Old Woman's every healthcare need!"

"I certainly hope so," Cunegonde replied. "We are trusting your guidance on this."

"And you can rely on me utterly," Milo declared. After finalizing the plans with Cunegonde, he ended the call, barely able to contain his glee. This was shaping up to be a banner month for sales. His bosses would be thrilled, and the commissions! Oh, the commissions!! With dollar signs dancing in his head, Milo put his BMW in drive and headed for home, cha-ching!!!

#

Cunegonde took a deep breath, after holding for an hour and listening to the incessant looped jingle:

Stay on hold,
Don't be bold,
Your health is gold,
At least that's what's said!

At CashCare Insurance,
We're never in a hurry,
Keep holding,
No worry!

Your money's our mission,
With every condition,
We find a way,
To make you pay!

So hold, dear caller,
As your wallet gets smaller,
With CashCare,
You're always in for a baller!

She finally heard a representative pick up.

"Thank you for calling CashCare, this is Michelle speaking. How may I assist you today?"

"Yes, hello Michelle. I'm calling on behalf of my friend who recently enrolled in your Advantage Plus plan. We submitted a prior authorization request for an ophthalmologist visit but it was denied. I was hoping you could help me understand why."

"Certainly, let me take a look at the request . . . ah yes, I see the issue. This particular specialist is out-of-network under your plan, so we cannot authorize coverage for her."

Cunegonde frowned. "Are there any in-network ophthalmologists in our area you can recommend instead?"

"Let me check . . . unfortunately we do not have any ophthalmology providers in your zip code at this time."

"None at all?" Cunegonde asked in disbelief.

"I'm afraid not. Your plan does offer out-of-network coverage at a higher cost to you, if you wish to see this specialist."

Cunegonde sighed. Higher costs were exactly what she hoped to avoid with the Advantage plan.

"Alright, thank you for clarifying. I'll discuss the options with my friend and get back to you if needed."

After hanging up, Cunegonde slumped back on the couch with a groan. The Old Woman peered over from her chair.

"No luck finding an ophthalmologist?"

"No. I knew this plan seemed too good to be true," Cunegonde grumbled.

The Old Woman consoled Cunegonde, "Don't be so gloomy! We'll find a way, just like we always do."

Cunegonde called Martin on his cell. "Martin, dear friend, The Medicare Advantage plan that Milo sold to the Old Woman has turned out to be as useful as a chocolate teapot. There's not a single ophthalmologist in her network!"

"Goodness gracious, Cunegonde, that's as absurd as a fish riding a bicycle!" Martin exclaimed. "Fear not, for I shall not stand idly by while our dear Old Woman suffers such injustice. I shall summon Milo forthwith and demand rectification!"

Cunegonde thanked him with an open heart. "Oh, Martin, you are our knight in shining armor! Pray, make haste."

"Fear not, fair Cunegonde, for I shall wield my phone like Excalibur and summon Milo to the battlefield of healthcare injustice!"

#

Martin called repeatedly for several days. Finally on the fifth day, Milo Vanderdendur answered. "Hello, you've reached Milo's Health Insurance Emporium, where we minimize your coverage to maximize our profits! How may I assist you today?"

Martin was so thrilled to finally have someone answer the phone that he almost forgot the reason for calling Milo. "Milo, this is Martin. We've got a bit of a pickle here. The Medicare Advantage plan you sold to our dear Old Woman has turned out to be about as useful as a screen door on a submarine. She can't even find an ophthalmologist in her network!"

"Ah, Martin, my good fellow!" Milo stirred up his enthusiasm. "I understand your concerns, but you see, these Advantage plans are like a golden ticket to healthcare paradise. It's in everyone's best interest to keep her locked into that plan tighter than a clam's grip on a pearl."

Martin began drumming his fingers on his desk . . . "Milo, Milo, Milo . . . Let us not pretend you're not frolicking through fields of dollar bills every time you sell one of those Advantage plans. But think of the poor Old Woman! She is as lost as a blind squirrel in a blizzard without proper eye care."

"Well, you make a valid point, Martin. I suppose we can't have the Old Woman stumbling around like a blindfolded bull in a china shop. But you see, these matters take time, like a fine wine aging in the cellar."

"Time? Milo, the Old Woman needs help now, not when she's old enough to qualify for Medicare Part Z! I implore you, don't make me resort to drastic measures."

"'Drastic measures,' you say? Oh, Martin, let's not resort to melodramatics! Rest assured; I'll do everything in my power to expedite the process. But remember, Rome wasn't built in a day, and neither is a properly functioning Medicare plan."

Martin was losing patience. "Milo, if this issue isn't resolved promptly, I'll have to pay you a personal visit."

"Now, now, let's not get our suspenders in a twist. A personal visit won't be necessary. I assure you; I'll take a look at the plan and see what loopholes—ahem, opportunities—ahem, exist."

"You'd better, Milo. It took me days to reach you. Off on a fishing trip on the Old Woman's money, were you? I'll hold you to your word. But remember, the clock is ticking, and time waits for no insurance salesman."

"Understood, Martin. I'll get right on it."

"Attaboy!" Martin hung up the phone with a sigh of half-disbelief and half-resignation.

Chapter 13

It is the greatest of all misfortunes to be at the mercy
of a man who is neither reasonable nor just. But it
is a greater misfortune still to be at the mercy of a
noble savage. ~ Voltaire

The jungle was dense and foreboding as Candide and Cacambo made their way down the muddy path in the old jeep. Strange animal calls echoed through the trees and the humidity was stifling. Candide wiped the sweat from his brow. "This jungle is nothing like the lovely gardens back home," he remarked.

Cacambo nodded, scanning the trees warily. "We must be vigilant, my friend. The jungle hides many dangers."

After several bone-jarring hours, they arrived at the Oreillon village. As the last rays of sunlight filtered through the canopy, they stumbled into a clearing. Crude huts dotted the area, surrounded by carved totem poles. Dark figures emerged, staring suspiciously.

Candide raised his hands in greeting. "We come in peace from the Jesuit hospital."

A muscular warrior stepped forward, face painted, hefting a spear. "What business have you here?"

"We wish to provide medical care," Candide explained. "Please, allow us to help your people."

The warrior scowled. "And spread your foreign beliefs? We want none of it." The villagers closed in, brandishing weapons. Candide's medical bag was ripped away.

"Wait!" Candide cried. "We mean no imposition! Just simple treatments." But his pleas fell on deaf ears.

Candide and Cacambo were seized, tightly bound, and brought before the imposing figure of the Oreillon Chief. He sat upon a throne of woven branches, adorned with rows of skulls, like a statue come to life—the very spirit of the jungle given human form. His stature was towering, and his muscles were like coiled serpents beneath his bronzed skin. His stern face was marked with intricate tattoos that snaked across his cheeks and forehead, merging into the headdress that crowned his head, a fierce-looking arrangement of feathers from exotic birds, bones from mysterious creatures, and bright beads made from polished seeds and stones. His eyes, a sharp shade of amber, locked onto Candide and Cacambo as they stood before him in the village square. The skulls on the throne stared at the pair blankly with their empty sockets.

"I ask you strangers, what brings you to our village?" The Chief growled; eyes narrowed in suspicion.

Candide's heart pounded as he scrambled for the right words. "We come in peace, Chief," he began nervously. "I am Candide, and this is my friend Cacambo. We only wish to help your people."

The Chief scrutinized them closely. "Help? How?"

"I am a doctor," Candide explained. "I can offer medical treatment to those in need." To demonstrate, he opened his satchel to reveal bandages and medicinal herbs.

"Help, you say?" the Chief rumbled. "How do I know you are not spies, meant to weaken us from within?"

Candide's mind raced, thinking of how to convince the wary Chief of their good intentions. He knew they must tread carefully here. One wrong move could turn the entire tribe against them.

"Great Chief," Candide said, hands spread wide in supplication. "I swear on my life we mean only to ease hardship where we find it. My friend and I devote ourselves to mending wounds, both of body and spirit."

The Chief snorted with derision. "Pretty words, pale one. But words alone will not sway me. Where are you and your companion from?"

Candide trembling, "From the Jesuit hospital on a medical mission."

The Chief, now infuriated, sputtered, "I hate the Jesuits. They pretend to do good while they plunder our land. A good Jesuit is a well boiled Jesuit."

Candide's shoulders slumped. What could he do or say to break through the Chief's distrust? If they could not get through to him, their mission here would be doomed.

Clearing his throat, Cacambo stepped forward, "Chief Oreillon, if I may?"

The Chief gave a curt nod.

Cacambo met the Chief's gaze, unwavering. "I was born of this land, of mothers and fathers not so unlike your own. I understand the old ways. Let us prove ourselves as friends to your people. Then you will see that our hearts are true."

The Chief pondered this in silence. Candide held his breath. After a moment, the Chief's lips curled into a smirk. "Very well.

You shall have a chance to prove yourselves. We will test your hearts at dinner. Now leave my presence."

Candide and Cacambo were dragged away by two guards to a hut in the outer skirt of the village. They huddled in the hut, their wrists and ankles bound tightly. Outside, the sounds of the jungle gave way to the bustle of the village preparing for the evening meal. The rich, smoky scent of roasting meat wafted under the door.

Candide's stomach rumbled. "I don't suppose they intend to feed their prisoners,"

Cacambo tested his bonds. "We need to get free before we end up as the main course."

"Candide, is that you?" a familiar voice called from the dark corner of the hut. Candide stared in astonishment as Pangloss emerged from the shadows, wrists and ankles bound, wiggling toward them. Candide could hardly believe his eyes; his old mentor, whom he thought had perished in the earthquake, was somehow alive before him in the middle of the Amazon jungle.

"Professor Pangloss! Is it really you?" Candide exclaimed.

"Indeed, my dear pupil!" Pangloss replied with a jovial tone. "What a fortuitous turn of events that our paths should cross again."

Pangloss went on to recount his miraculous tale of survival since the earthquake. He spoke of being swept out to sea by the tsunami, floating in the giant rubber ducky for days, and eventually washing up on the shores of Brazil. Candide and Cacambo listened intently, marveling at Pangloss's optimism and faith despite such harrowing circumstances.

"Remarkable, truly remarkable!" Candide said, "and what brings you to these parts now?"

"Ah, I have been wandering through the rainforest, observing its splendors and studying its native inhabitants," Pangloss continued. "Imagine my surprise when I stumbled upon this village and found myself taken captive by the Oreillon tribe. Fortune has allowed our paths to intertwine once again, bringing us together for whatever grand adventures may come next," Pangloss declared with a happy smile.

Candide felt his spirits lift at having his dear mentor back by his side once again, with Pangloss's eternal optimism bolstering him. However, his cheer began to fade as the reality of their situation set in. They were imprisoned in the depths of the Amazon rainforest, at the mercy of a tribe of cannibals, with no clear means of escape.

Candide turned to Pangloss. "Teacher, how can you remain so positive given our dire circumstances? We know not where we are headed nor what further perils may await."

"My dear Candide," Pangloss replied in a soothing voice, "one must have faith that all occurs for good reason. Each twist of fate leads us toward greater understanding."

Candide frowned, unsatisfied by this vague assurance. After all they had suffered, he found his old mentor's blind optimism increasingly frustrating.

Sensing Candide's resentment, Pangloss wiggled closer to Candide. "There are realities in this world we cannot control. What we can control is how we respond. I choose to face each moment with hope and grace."

With a sigh, Candide nodded and managed to put on a weak smile. "You're right, of course," he conceded. "We must make the best of whatever comes next."

Pangloss beamed proudly at his pupil. Together, master and apprentice continued into the night, spirits lifted once more. Though unsure of what lay ahead, they moved forward with faith.

Late in the night, Candide stirred awake to the sound of drums beating steadily outside. For a moment, he forgot where he was. Then it all came rushing back: the remote village, the suspicious Oreillons, and their impending ritual. The guards arrived at the hut, untied Candide, Cacambo, and Pangloss, and motioned with their spears for the trio to follow. Candide's stomach was in knots, but he forced himself to stand tall. He swore he would face whatever came with courage and dignity.

They were led to the center of the village, where a large fire blazed under a huge boiling cauldron. All around them, the Oreillons were adorned in elaborate costumes and painted faces. They chanted and danced with the hypnotic intensity of a steady drumbeat.

Boil and toil in the jungle night,
Cooking strangers by firelight.
Laugh and jest, for we are keen,
To feast on dishes never seen.

With herbs and spices, we'll prepare,
A foreign feast beyond compare.
Sorry, dear guests, you won't get a bite,
You're the course for our delight!

In the flickering firelight, Candide caught the Chief's eye. The man's expression was impassive, his eyes transfixed at the large cauldron in the center of the fiery circle.

Off to either side of the throne sat the royal family, all staring intently at the trio. Closest to the Chief was his elderly mother, who seemed unperturbed by the tumult of the ritual and untouched by its ferocity. Her sightless eyes, like pearls, reflected the fire's glow beneath the cauldron.

Three warriors tied Candide, Cacambo, and Pangloss each to a post near the cauldron and bared their chests. Their skins glistened, sweat beading from the heat of the boiling cauldron. As the chanting reached fever pitch and the drumbeat quickened, the chief unsheathed an obsidian knife, held it aloft, and stepped toward Candide. A shiver raced down Candide's spine as he realized what fate awaited. Candide steeled himself, prepared to meet his destiny.

Pangloss, however, seemed undeterred by the sinister display. He straightened his back and addressed the Chief in a clarion voice, resonating over the drums. "Great Chief Oreillon," he began, "we come before you not as enemies, but as friends and healers. We can restore your mother's sight."

With a raised hand, the Chief signaled for the drums to halt. He studied Pangloss, then turned to Candide and Cacambo.

"Show us the healing power you speak of," his deep voice echoed through the depths of the jungle.

Pangloss responded, "Candide has the healing power of sight."

The village fell into hushed silence, all eyes fixated on the small group by the cauldron. The Chief glanced between the trio and his mother, the elderly woman with sightless eyes. He scoffed at the suggestion but was intrigued enough to entertain it.

"Prove this claim," the Chief demanded, motioning toward his mother. "Restore her sight, and perhaps you will earn your freedom."

Pangloss continued his offer. "Chief of the Oreillons, you will not be disappointed. But first we have to prepare ourselves to perform such a miracle."

Still racked by his near-death experience, Candide glanced helplessly at Pangloss, who gave him an encouraging nod and whispered, "Remember how you performed your first cataract surgery in Haiti."

Candide nodded, regaining his composure. Memories of Haiti began to flood back: the humid operating conditions in a makeshift hospital and the cataract surgery that took hours to complete.

"First," Pangloss said to the Chief, "we need clean water, bandages, and some herbs from the forest. We will need a long needle and your obsidian knife."

"Release the prisoners and lend assistance," the Chief commanded. "One wrong move and the cauldron awaits you three Jesuits," he warned.

The Oreillons promptly complied, intrigued by the unfolding spectacle. Candide, recalling the operation he had performed in Haiti, instructed Cacambo to gather the necessary herbs and instruments.

The Chief's warriors released Candide from the post and led him to their sightless matriarch. Her pupils were pearly white from cataracts. With Cacambo as an interpreter, Candide asked her to drink a soporific soup made from herbs. After she fell asleep, she was laid flat on her back on a large table. Candide sterilized a long needle and the obsidian blade in the fire. He washed the matriarch's eyes with boiled water from the cauldron, after it had cooled. With the entire village watching in silence, Pangloss and Cacambo stood on either side holding the body steady on the table as Candide stood at the head. Cacambo murmured a prayer in Guaraní. Pangloss smiled at Candide and mouthed, "It's going to be beautiful."

Candide gently opened her right eye with his left hand. Cacambo handed him the obsidian knife. The blade slid into the eye easily, like a hot knife cutting through butter. The heat from the blade cauterized the bleeding instantaneously. Candide inserted the needle into the eye through the incision. He maneuvered the needle to push the cataract deep into the eye, away from the line of sight. In less than three minutes, the operation was over.

The matriarch remained in deep sleep throughout the procedure, her breathing steady and unlabored. The villagers had gathered closer, their collective breath held in anticipation as Candide stepped back, his face a mask of concentration. Cacambo cleaned the wound with more of the cooled water from the cauldron, and Pangloss applied a poultice of medicinal herbs before bandaging the eye.

Candide repeated the procedure on the second eye, under the villagers' intense gaze, amid deafening silence. After completing the operation, he sighed softly and stepped back to let the elder woman rest. Hours ticked by while the tribe awaited their matriarch's awakening. Throughout this time, the Oreillon Chief sat almost motionless on his throne, closely watching every move the trio made.

Candide, Pangloss, and Cacambo were given food and water but remained under the vigilant watch of the Chief's guards. The air was thick with tension and curiosity; none of the Oreillons had ever witnessed such a ritual before. As the first golden rays of the sun began to sweep over the village, the matriarch stirred. A murmur arose among the Oreillons as the Chief approached the makeshift operating table. Candide removed the bandages; her eyelids fluttered open. Candide and his companions held their breath, praying in silence that their efforts had not been in vain.

The elderly woman blinked several times, her vision clearing. Then, with a sudden gasp, she sat up and focused on the faces around her. A look of wonder came over her as she reached out to touch the face of her son, the Chief, seeing him clearly for the first time in many years.

The crowd burst into cheers as they witnessed the miracle. The Chief, his eyes glistening with unshed tears, embraced his mother. Turning to Candide and his friends, he spoke in a voice filled with emotion. "You have restored more than sight; you have given back life to her eyes and hope to our people." With this declaration, the Chief ordered their bonds be cut and proclaimed them friends of the Oreillon tribe. The village erupted in celebration, their chants now a jubilant chorus honoring the newly anointed healers.

Candide, overwhelmed by the turn of events, could scarcely believe the results of his own handiwork. He had gone from the precipice of death to the pinnacle of reverence in a matter of hours. Pangloss, meanwhile, wore a smile that seemed to say, "All is for the best, in the best of all possible worlds."

The Chief's mother, now able to see her people and the beauty of the land with her own eyes, was a testament to their goodwill and skill. Stories would be told of their miraculous healing hands for generations to come. In return for their service, the Oreillons showered them with gifts—vibrant feathers from exotic birds, beautifully woven tapestries, and golden trinkets—showing the gratitude of a people whose heartache had been transformed into joy.

As night fell and the festivities waned, the three men sat by a newly kindled fire, reflecting on the events that had unfolded. Their jeep was parked at the edge of the village, now loaded with the gifts and treasures given to them by the Oreillons. The air hummed with the residual energy of the day's celebrations, as nocturnal life murmured softly in the background. In the quiet aftermath of the day's events, Candide found himself deep in thought. Cacambo, always pragmatic and resourceful, checked their supplies, ensuring everything was secure for their journey the next day.

Pangloss, ever the philosopher, stared into the flickering flames. "It is remarkable," Pangloss began, his voice a melodic cadence that seemed to dance with the fire's crackle, "how our actions here have changed not only our fates but those of an entire tribe."

Candide nodded in agreement. "Indeed, Professor. But it is a change brought about by fortune and necessity, rather than virtue or vice. It seems to me that we are merely leaves caught in a tempest, flung about by forces beyond our control."

Pangloss chuckled softly. "You may say so, dear Candide, yet it does not diminish the joy we have brought this day. Nor does it tarnish the skill you have displayed in such a grave situation."

"And what of tomorrow?" Cacambo interjected, his hands still busy with their supplies. "We have found favor here, but we cannot forget our ultimate goal—to find our own paradise and to reunite Candide with Cunegonde. We should not tarry too long in one place, no matter how welcoming."

Candide gazed into the flames, considering Cacambo's words. The fire cast a warm glow on his face. "You are right, my friend. We shall leave tomorrow. Our journey is far from over."

Chapter 14

*Doctors are men who prescribe medicines of which
they know little, to cure diseases of which they know
less, in human beings of whom they know nothing.*
~ Voltaire

After Martin's timely phone call to Milo Vanderdendur, the health insurance salesman, the Old Woman was enrolled in a traditional PPO Medicare plan with an extensive physician network and a comprehensive drug formulary. However, the pressure in her eyes remained persistently elevated due to glaucoma, and eyedrops had failed to reduce it. As a result, she was referred to Dr Glaukomflecken, the world-renowned glaucoma specialist.

In the grand, almost palatial office of Dr. Glaukomflecken, one wall was adorned with diplomas, certificates, awards, and photos with both foreign and domestic dignitaries, showcasing his accomplishments and fame as one of the world's premier ophthalmologists. The other walls were lined with expensive artwork and featured a large portrait of the doctor himself, holding a giant eyeball and gazing into the distance as if contemplating the mysteries of an expanding ocular universe. Below the portrait, a small plaque read, "Owned and operated by Usurious Ventures: Exploiting Opportunity with Don Issachar Private Equity LLC."

Cunegonde and the Old Woman settled into plush leather chairs far too large for their frames. The air was thick with the scent of polished wood, and leather-bound books lined the shelves in the lavish waiting room. Time passed in a lull of soft but incessant classical music.

"It's a good thing Martin made that call," Cunegonde whispered, her eyes roving over the opulence. "I wouldn't even know where to start in a place like this."

The Old Woman nodded, adjusting the spectacles on her nose with a wince. "Let's hope Dr. Glaukomflecken can do something for these blasted eyes of mine."

The receptionist, whose expressionless face suggested she had witnessed many a spectacle in this office, intoned, "Dr. Glaukomflecken will see you now." She gestured toward the towering doors, behind which lay the inner sanctum of the great eye wizard. As Cunegonde and the Old Woman entered, they were met by Dr. Glaukomflecken himself, an imposing figure perched behind a desk that could double as a small stage. He wore a pristine white coat, accented by a monocle that magnified the eye behind it, making it appear disproportionately large.

Dr. Glaukomflecken stood so tall that he could easily retrieve books from the top shelf without a ladder. He extended a hand as meticulously manicured as the bonsai gracing one corner of his ostentatious office. His grip was firm, and his smile was practiced to perfection. Nearly bald, the few short, fuzzy hairs that remained seemed to catch the brilliant sheen from the overhead lights, casting a halo around him—the Saint of Sight.

"Dear Old Woman, I've been reviewing your case," Dr. Glaukomflecken said in a confident and soothing voice. "While your situation is indeed complex, I am optimistic we can improve your condition." He motioned for them to follow him into the examination room. "Please, take a seat here," he directed the Old Woman to an exam chair outfitted with various instruments and armatures. "We shall commence with a series of tests to ascertain the extent of your condition."

For the next hour, the Old Woman underwent a battery of examinations and tests. Lights flickered in her eyes, lenses clicked into place before her vision, and puffs of air gently blew onto her eyeballs. Dr. Glaukomflecken hummed to himself as he peered deeply into her eyes through his instruments and examined the images on the computer screens, his expression one of intense focus. Cunegonde watched on nervously.

When the examination was over, Dr. Glaukomflecken leaned back and said, "Ah, my dear Old Woman," his voice resonating with an assuredness that only years of being unconditionally revered could bestow. "After perusing your past medical records and examining your eyes with a meticulousness that lesser mortals can only dream of, it appears the inflammation in your eyes has receded, bowing to the might of the steroid drops prescribed by your previous eye doctor."

Dr. Glaukomflecken leaned closer to the Old Woman, the eye behind his monocle appearing ever larger. "However, your eye pressure has begun to rise, a clear act of defiance that my expertise shall not tolerate," he declared. "We will need to discuss surgical options, as medications alone seem inadequate in taming this rebellious pressure."

The Old Woman swallowed hard; her throat dried at the mention of surgery. Cunegonde reached out and squeezed her hand.

"There are several procedures we can consider," Dr. Glaukomflecken continued, pulling out a chart and a laser pointer. "One option is a trabeculectomy, where we fashion a new drainage passage for the outflow of aqueous humor to release the built-up pressure in your eye. Another is the implantation of a tiny device, a glaucoma drainage implant, that helps maintain acceptable levels of intraocular pressure." He explained each procedure with enthusiasm usually reserved for discussing a Monet painting or analyzing a Mahler symphony. The Old Woman listened intently, feeling like a mere spectator in a theater where her fate was the main performance, with Dr. Glaukomflecken orchestrating as the maestro. His words, while informative, weighed heavily on her chest.

"The success rates for these surgeries are quite high," Dr. Glaukomflecken assured her, noting the concern on her face. "Of course, as with any surgical procedure, there are inherent risks, but I will ensure we take all necessary precautions."

The Old Woman, clearly overwhelmed, ventured, "Is there no simpler way? Perhaps a potion, or an ancient ritual performed under the moonlight?"

"My dear lady," Dr. Glaukomflecken replied with a chuckle, "while your suggestions tickle my fancy, we must adhere to the high standards of modern medicine, a field in which I am an undisputed titan. Surgery is our best option, and I assure you, in my capable hands, it will be nothing short of miraculous."

The Old Woman pondered this, her mind racing. "And if I may inquire, Dr. Glaukomflecken," she asked, "what would you recommend? What would you do if I were your mother?"

There was a brief pause as the doctor regarded her through his magnified eye before responding with a thoughtful nod. "If you were my mother," he said slowly, "I would opt for the glaucoma drainage implant, specifically one of my own designs, the Glaukomflecken shunt. It's state-of-the-art, less invasive than a trabeculectomy, and has an excellent track record of achieving the lowest possible eye pressure."

The Old Woman felt a measure of relief at his recommendation; the idea of something less invasive appealed to her. Cunegonde nodded and gave her hand another reassuring squeeze.

"Let's proceed with that then," she said, her voice stronger than she felt. "When can we schedule the surgery?"

Checking his computer screen with a few quick keystrokes, Dr Glaukomflecken responded, "I think we can fit you in next week."

In the aftermath of the surgery, the inflammation resurged in the Old Woman's eyes, now as red and puffy as ever, as if she had taken up onion chopping as a profession. Her vision was as clear as mud puddles following a heavy rainstorm.

"Dr. Glaukomflecken," Cunegonde began, her voice laced with worry, "her eyes are more inflamed than ever, and it seems like the pressure has dramatically dropped—to zero. It's like there's no fight left in them at all."

Dr. Glaukomflecken, seated regally in his throne-like chair, peered at them through his monocle, his eye magnifying with each visit. "Ah, but of course," he said with a wave of his hand. "This is all part of the grand plan. Zero pressure, you see, is an indication that we've managed the glaucoma effectively. Your eyes are now perfectly relaxed. Why, they're practically meditating!"

The Old Woman, squinting through the discomfort, tried to muster a smile. "I was hoping for a bit more vision, less enlightenment, to be honest."

Cunegonde added, "Yes, we were aiming for her to see the world, not for her eyes to achieve nirvana."

Dr. Glaukomflecken chuckled. "My dear ladies, you must understand that the path to ocular rejuvenation is much like a dance. Sometimes, one must step back to leap forward. Your eyes are merely pausing, gathering strength for the grand performance yet to come."

The Old Woman leaned forward, curiosity piqued despite her unease. "And what if this performance ends with a standing ovation of more inflammation? Do we take a bow or run for the exit?"

"Ah," Dr. Glaukomflecken exclaimed, his voice brimming with assurance, "but that is the beauty of it! Should the need arise, I am ready to encore with additional treatments, more surgeries! My repertoire is endless, and my hands are steady. Fear not, for I am the conductor of this ocular symphony, and we shall indeed end on a high note!"

Cunegonde shot back, "Let's just hope it's not a high note of permanent darkness. I hear that's a tough act to follow."

Dr. Glaukomflecken, unfazed, made a grand, sweeping gesture towards the door. "Worry not, for I have never left the stage without applause. You shall see, in more ways than one. Now, go forth and rest. Allow the magic of my work to manifest."

#

One week later, back in the opulent office of Dr. Glaukomflecken, where the air was thick with what the doctor considered the scent of success, Cunegonde and the Old Woman presented themselves once more. Now navigating the world as if she were a blind mouse, the Old Woman had developed retinal detachments in both eyes, a turn of events that made their previous concerns seem almost quaint.

"Dr. Glaukomflecken," Cunegonde began, her patience wearing as thin as the doctor's hairline, "while we're thrilled the pressure in her eyes could rival that of a vacuum, it seems her retinas didn't get the memo and have decided to part ways with the rest of her eyeballs."

Dr. Glaukomflecken, self-confidence personified, adjusted his monocle. "Ah, but my dear Cunegonde, let us not dwell on the negatives. The inflammation has indeed improved, and the eye pressure remains a marvel of modern medicine—zero! As for the detachments, it's as if her eyes have achieved a state of perfect tranquility, a rare serene repose seldom seen."

The Old Woman chimed in, "Tranquil, yes, but I was rather hoping to see with them as well. This detachment my eyes have attained is rather inconvenient."

Cunegonde sigh. "Yes, it's all well and good that they're re-laxed, but if they're too laid-back to actually see, it seems we've gone from the frying pan into the fire."

Unbothered by the gravity of the situation, Dr. Glaukom-flecken proclaimed, "Fear not, for my part in this grand ocular odyssey is complete. I have tamed the wild pressures of the eye, a feat for which I shall no doubt be remembered. As for the retinal detachment, I shall refer you to my esteemed colleague, Dr. Dru-sen, a retinal specialist who will be thrilled to continue this historic journey of sight."

The Old Woman, squinting in an attempt to visualize the doctor, asked, "And will this specialist be as . . . enthusiastic about our predicament as you are?"

"Ah, he is a man of great skill and, while perhaps not quite as gifted in the art of conversation as myself, I assure you, he is more than capable of reattaching what has been detached. Consider him an artist who specializes in the finer details, while I, dear ladies, am the visionary who sets the stage."

Suppressing her frustration, Cunegonde quipped, "Let's hope his vision extends beyond his ego. We wouldn't want the Old

Woman's eyes to become a permanent exhibit in the museum of medical mysteries."

The Old Woman sighed. "Let's hope this Dr. Drusen can re-attach what is detached, or I'll be reduced to navigating the world by cane alone."

"Have faith, dear lady," Dr. Glaukomflecken implored. "While the road ahead may be blurred for now, you have the two finest ocular experts in the land on your side. Your eyes could ask for no better champions!"

Cunegonde took the Old Woman's arm. "Well then, we'd best be on our way. It seems the curtain's about to rise on Act Two of this ocular odyssey."

Dr. Glaukomflecken replied with a booming laugh that filled the room, "Ah, Cunegonde, ever the wit. Rest assured, the tale of the Old Woman's eyes shall end not in mystery, but in triumph. Now, off you go to the specialist; Dr. Drusen awaits! Indeed, break a leg!" he called out as they departed. "For your eyes, and your vision, I shall cheer from the front row!"

Chapter 15

"Our people [in El Dorado] are not more happy than others," said the old man, "but they are equally happy." ~ Voltaire

The jeep jolted violently as it struck another rut in the jungle road, nearly tossing Candide from his seat. Clutching the roll bar, his knuckles whitened with tension as he glanced over at Pangloss.

"So, Pangloss," he shouted over the roar of the engine and the screeching of birds, "after narrowly escaping being boiled and eaten, do you still maintain that this is the *best of all possible worlds?*"

Pangloss, unperturbed by Candide's sarcastic tone, replied as usual. "But of course, dear boy! Our brush with danger was merely another step along life's grand adventure." Pangloss continued to prattle on, waxing poetic about the jungle's beauty and the intricate tapestry of life. Meanwhile, Candide tuned him out, his gaze fixed on the dense foliage rushing past. It all looked the same—an endless sea of green, a blur of danger.

Cacambo laughed as he swerved around another pothole, jostling his passengers. "I have to agree with Candide on this one, Pangloss. No offense, but your optimism seems a bit overzealous considering we were nearly cannibalized!"

Straightening his rumpled jacket and pushing his glasses up his nose, Pangloss huffed, "Overzealous? Nonsense! One must never abandon hope, my friends, no matter how dire the situation."

"Hope is one thing, but your outright denial of reality concerns me," Cacambo replied, raising an eyebrow. "Sometimes life does take a turn for the worse, and there's no shame in admitting that."

Pangloss shook his head. "No, no, you've got it all wrong! Each twist and turn of life has its purpose. We escaped the Oreillons for a reason—to continue our journey, enriched by the experience!"

"Well, I'm just glad we survived thanks to quick thinking and fast feet," Candide said, "not because of some grand plan."

Cacambo nodded. "Too true. We have only ourselves to rely on out here," he said, patting the worn steering wheel. "And this heap of junk, bless its heart," he added, just as they bounced over another rut. The jungle seemed less oppressive now, filled with their banter as they headed back to the Jesuit hospital, laden with gifts from the Oreillons.

Candide gazed out at the vibrant greenery flowing past, so unlike the manicured gardens of his hometown. Despite the hazards, he had to admit there was a wild beauty to the untamed wilderness surrounding them.

"Pangloss . . ." Candide began, but before he could ask his question, the ground vanished beneath them. Candide's stomach dropped as the jeep plunged into empty space. "Not again!" he yelled, gripping his seat in panic. The vehicle had fallen into a sinkhole, taking its passengers with it. He clutched the roll bar tightly, his knuckles whitening. "You've got to be kidding me! Can't we just catch a break for once?"

Despite Candide's rising panic, Pangloss remained infuriatingly calm as the jeep plunged into the sinkhole. "My dear fellow," he declared, "every experience, however harrowing, presents an opportunity for wisdom!"

As the jeep descended, Cacambo, struggling to steer the nearly airborne vehicle, muttered a short prayer in Guaraní. They crashed through loose dirt and roots, sending debris raining down around them.

Candide braced himself for the impending impact. The jeep crashed onto the muddy floor with a tremendous splash, jolting the trio violently. For a moment, everything was still and quiet as they caught their breath. A dim light streamed in from above, casting eerie shadows on the walls of their earthen prison. The sound of running water echoed throughout the cavernous chamber.

Cacambo clambered out of the jeep and switched on a flashlight to illuminate the cavernous space. "Well, we're not dead. That's something," he remarked, his boots squelching through the mud as he approached the edge of a subterranean river that flowed along the bottom of the sinkhole.

Pangloss followed, crawling out and dusting the dirt from his clothes. "Look at this place! Isn't it marvelous? The intricate architecture of nature is truly astounding!" he exclaimed, his eyes wide with wonder.

Candide stumbled out last. "Marvelous isn't exactly the word I'd use," he grumbled, peering warily at the steep walls that towered over them. "Now how do we get out of here?" His flashlight beam danced across the slick walls of the sinkhole, failing to reveal even the hint of a handhold.

"We'll have to follow this river," Cacambo suggested, pointing downstream where the murky water disappeared into the darkness. "It has to lead somewhere."

As they approached the subterranean river, its gentle flow had an inviting gleam, even in the absence of natural light. The surrounding walls glistened with moisture and were dotted with strange luminescent fungi, casting a surreal glow over the scene. "Looks like this is our way out," Cacambo declared, his voice faintly echoing. "Following the current is sure to lead us somewhere beyond these walls."

Candide and Pangloss followed closely, straining their eyes in the dim, otherworldly light. Around them, bizarre rock formations and tangled roots created an environment that felt more like an alien landscape than the familiar earth above.

"Good heavens, it's so dark," Candide muttered, his voice tinged with unease. "We could get lost down here forever!"

"Nonsense, dear boy!" Pangloss replied, his tone brimming with conviction. "Difficulties are merely opportunities in disguise. Have courage!"

Candide hurried to keep up with Cacambo's energetic pace, nearly tripping over roots and loose rocks. His flashlight beam swept erratically across the uneven terrain as he struggled to watch his footing.

"Slow down, will you?" Candide called out to Cacambo, his voice reverberating in the cavernous space. "We have no idea where we're going down here!"

Cacambo gave him a hard look. "Unless you have a map, following the river is our only choice," he retorted.

"I'd prefer a map," Candide muttered under his breath.

Pangloss sidled up beside him, as chipper as ever. "Maps are useless things, my dear Candide! The joy is in the journey, not the destination."

Candide bit back an irritated reply, resigning himself to let Pangloss turn their aimless wandering into some grand philosophical quest.

Up ahead, Cacambo let out an excited shout. "Look, a tunnel! I wonder where it leads?" Without waiting for a response, he scrambled into the dark opening. Candide and Pangloss hurried after him, their hearts pounding. As they emerged from the tunnel, the sudden transition from darkness to light dazzled them. Water sloshed around their ankles as they looked around, bewildered, only to find themselves in a landscape unlike any they had ever seen before.

"By the whiskers of Voltaire! Where in the world are we now?" Candide exclaimed, squinting against the brilliant sunlight that reflected off the crystalline waters.

Cacambo, equally astonished, uttered, "It looks like some sort of paradise!"

Lush greenery lined the riverbanks while strange, colorful birds fluttered overhead. In the distance, mountains towered, gleaming as if made of solid gold.

Pangloss clasped his hands in delight. "Remarkable! It seems our unplanned detour has brought us to a hidden corner of Eden!"

Cacambo led them along the winding riverbank, ducking under hanging vines and pushing aside giant leaves. The thick jungle teemed with life; brightly feathered birds chattered from the canopy overhead, while strange rodents scurried through the underbrush. Gradually, the dense vegetation began to thin.

Up ahead, Candide spotted an expanse of cleared land. "Look there!" he exclaimed, pointing. Nestled between the mountains lay a glittering city, whose towers and domes appeared to be made entirely of gold.

Pangloss let out an excited cry. "My dear fellows, could it possibly be? Unless I'm very much mistaken, we've stumbled upon the lost city of Eldorado!"

"Eldorado?" Cacambo scratched his head, looking on with disbelief. "But isn't that just a myth?"

"Clearly not!" Pangloss declared, gesturing toward the city. "Here—laid out before us—is tangible proof that the stories were true."

Candide shook his head in amazement. "Incredible. Of all the places we could have ended up, to think it's the fabled city of gold." His eyes widened as he took in the splendor surrounding them. The very air seemed to shimmer with opulence. "Well, this is not at all what I had pictured for a mythical land," he remarked. "But I daresay the legends hardly did it justice!"

Cacambo nodded, visibly impressed by the riches on display. As a seasoned traveler, he was no stranger to wealth—yet even he had to admit that Eldorado exceeded anything he'd ever encountered.

As the three of them waded ashore, they were met by a procession of Eldoradians, bedecked in robes woven from strands of pure gold and adorned with jewels. The inhabitants greeted them with a mixture of curiosity and delight, offering warm smiles and outstretched hands.

Pangloss stepped forward and addressed their hosts. "My dear people! What a delight to make your acquaintance. Truly, your land surpasses every notion of paradise."

An Eldoradian stepped forward. "We bid you welcome, travelers. Allow me the honor of being your guide. Please accept the hospitality of Eldorado during your stay here." His voice was warm, touched by a musical lilt.

Candide bowed graciously. "You honor us, good sir. We are deeply grateful for this opportunity to experience your wondrous realm."

As the Eldoradian ushered them along a shimmering boulevard paved with gold, Candide could scarcely believe his eyes. Their host led the trio through the resplendent city, where golden spires reached toward the heavens and fountains cascaded with jewels instead of water. Diamonds and gold dust scattered in the streets sparkled like a carpet of stars under their feet.

Surrounding each opulent structure were verdant gardens, a riot of colors with flowers in hues Candide had never seen before. The trees bore fruits that glowed as if lit from within, perfuming the air with their sweet scent.

As Candide and Cacambo hastily stuffed their pockets with diamonds and gold dust, their Eldoradian host smiled with amusement. "Please, my friends, there is no need to labor so frantically," he said with a chuckle. "Here in Eldorado, gold and gems are as common as stones and sand in your world. We mainly use them for decoration, as they hold no real value to us."

Candide and Cacambo exchanged embarrassed glances before reluctantly emptying their bulging pockets. The riches fell back onto the path with a gentle clink. Overcome with amusement at their own folly, they both laughed.

Pangloss nodded. "A lesson in value and abundance! What is precious in one place may be plentiful in another. Truly this is the best of all possible worlds!"

With lighter pockets and enlightened minds, Candide, Cacambo, and Pangloss followed their Eldoradian host deeper into the heart of the legendary realm. As they walked along marble avenues lined with intricate fountains, Pangloss turned to their guide with an inquisitive look.

"Pray tell, good sir, what do the Eldoradians occupy themselves with in such a utopia?" Pangloss asked. "Surely, with all this abundance, there must be pursuits to feed the mind and spirit?"

With a warm smile, the Eldoradian responded, "An astute question, my friend. Indeed, while we lack nothing in material wealth, we find far greater riches in creativity, learning, and community." He gestured broadly at the magnificent buildings around them. "Many here devote themselves to the sciences and the arts, pushing the boundaries of knowledge. Others provide guidance and wisdom to our youth, while some prefer to tend the land and revere the beauty of nature."

Pangloss nodded thoughtfully. "A diverse tapestry of pursuits, yet all aimed at bettering oneself and others. Fascinating!"

His curiosity piqued, Candide spoke up, "But with such prosperity, what motivates people to work at all?"

"Purpose and meaning, dear Candide," the Eldoradian replied. "We find fulfillment in using our gifts to uplift our society. Labor is pleasure when it aligns with one's calling."

"Remarkable!" Pangloss exclaimed. "You have built a true utopia, unburdened by the vices of greed and envy. We indeed have much to learn from your ways."

Their guide smiled with humility. "And we from yours, in time. But come, the day wanes. Let us continue our journey."

The trio continued through the bustling streets of Eldorado's capital, soaking in the sights and sounds. Grand temples with sweeping archways lined the avenues, and in the public squares, musicians filled the air with melodies both haunting and joyful, while dancers interpreted their rhythms with fluid grace.

"How do you manage to maintain such a paradise?" Candide asked, his face alight with curiosity.

The Eldoradian smiled and gestured towards the lively streets. "It is through a deep reverence for life itself," he explained. "Our society cherishes each individual's contribution, ensuring that everyone finds meaning and joy in their endeavors. This collective respect fosters a natural harmony."

Candide's gaze followed the Eldoradian's hand as he took in the scenes around them. Children laughed and played in the central plaza, engaged in a game of their own invention. Nearby, a group of artists painted vivid murals on the walls, their expressions focused and serene.

"Here in Eldorado, we honor the interconnectedness of all living beings," the Eldoradian continued. "Each person contributes their unique gifts, which are celebrated by the community. We strive to live in unity with each other and in balance with the natural world."

Candide nodded, his understanding deepening. "So, by valuing each individual and promoting cooperation over competition, conflict simply doesn't arise."

"Precisely," the Eldoradian replied, his voice firm with conviction. "When everyone is free to thrive in their own way, the collective benefit is profound. The tapestry of society becomes a work of art, woven from many diverse threads."

Pangloss nodded in appreciation. "A truly enlightened approach to existence," he remarked. "It seems that in Eldorado, the pursuit of individual fulfillment has elevated collective well-being to unprecedented heights."

As Pangloss, Candide, Cacambo, and their Eldoradian guide strolled through the city of Eldorado, they encountered a remarkable sight. The streets were filled with shimmering golden carriages gliding silently through the air in perfect synchrony. There were no traffic lights, car noises, sirens, or horns honking, and no exhaust fumes—just clean, effortless transportation.

Candide's eyes widened in awe as one of the sleek vehicles floated past just overhead. "Incredible!" he exclaimed. "How do they work?"

"Using dark energy," the guide explained. "Our scientists long ago unlocked the secrets of harnessing dark energy from the expansion of the Universe as our primary source of power."

Pangloss stroked his chin thoughtfully as another carriage drifted by. "Remarkable. The ingenuity of your people is truly impressive. I can only imagine what other innovations you have devised."

As they walked, Pangloss, Candide, and Cacambo continued to gaze in wonder at the buildings of Eldorado. The architecture blended seamlessly with the natural landscape, featuring sweeping arches, domed rooftops, and vine-covered columns, all crafted from golden stone and marble.

Towering spires stretched elegantly toward the sky, their surfaces intricately carved with geometric patterns and inlaid with shimmering mosaics. Candide craned his neck to take in the sheer height of the spires, which were topped with gleaming crystals that caught and refracted the sunlight.

"Astounding," Pangloss marveled. "The craftsmanship is exquisite. And yet the buildings feel entirely organic, as if they sprouted naturally from the earth itself."

Their Eldoradian guide gave them a warm smile. "We have learned to build in harmony with the land. Our structures are not only infused with life-force but also with cosmic energy."

At last, the trio arrived at their accommodations for the evening. An elegant tower rose before them, its smooth golden walls lavishly adorned with intricate designs. The setting sun set the carvings ablaze, illuminating every detail.

"It's... It's...," Candide stammered, overwhelmed. "Why, it's just beyond words!" Utterly enraptured by the building's beauty, he finally exclaimed, "I've never laid eyes on its equal."

Pangloss clasped a hand on Candide's shoulder. "Now this is a structure worthy of housing such esteemed guests! Eldorado's riches know no bounds."

Their guide gave a gracious bow. "We hope you find it most comfortable during your time here in Eldorado."

Candide stepped through the towering golden doors into the interior of the lavish accommodations, his eyes wide with amazement. The high-ceilinged foyer was paneled with elaborate frescoes, and a massive crystal chandelier cast prismatic rainbows across the shimmering marble floors.

"Goodness gracious!" Candide exclaimed, turning in a slow circle to take it all in. "I've stayed in some fancy places before, but this takes the cake!"

The Eldoradian guide smiled modestly, amused at Candide's reaction. "I'm glad you find it to your liking, though I must apologize if the accommodations are not quite up to your expectations."

"Not up to our expectations?" Candide replied, incredulous. "My dear sir, I've never seen such opulence and grandeur! Back home, a place like this would indeed be reserved for royalty!"

Cacambo let out an appreciative whistle as he inspected a solid gold statue in an alcove. "Simply remarkable. The craftsmanship here surpasses anything I've ever seen."

Candide ran his fingers over the smooth marble countertops and intricate mosaic tiles, still struggling to believe that this was to be their lodging. He pondered what other wonders Eldorado might hold if this was merely a taste of their hospitality. He could hardly wait to find out.

Pangloss chuckled, shaking his head in amazement. "My dear friends, this is beyond anything we could have imagined in our world! Why, back home, a place such as this would be purely the stuff of legends!"

Cacambo nodded as he gazed upward at the soaring ceilings adorned with intricate carvings. "Indeed, I've never encountered such luxury and artistry in all my travels around the world. You Eldoradians have truly outdone yourselves in creating such grandeur." He turned to their guide with sincere appreciation. "Good sir, your hospitality humbles us."

The Eldoradian replied with a warm smile, "It brings us great joy to share the bounty of Eldorado with new friends. Tomorrow, I will escort you, my honored guests, to an audience with our king. Please, relax and make yourselves at home here."

As he excused himself, Candide sank onto a plush velvet sofa with a contented sigh. "Well, my friends, I'd say our fortunes have certainly taken a turn for the better, wouldn't you?"

Pangloss chuckled in agreement. "Quite right, Candide! Why, if this is how we are received as strangers, just imagine the delights that await us when we are presented to the king!"

The trio shared an excited laugh, their eagerness palpable as they anticipated discovering more of Eldorado's wonders. For now, they would savor the generous hospitality of this paradise.

Chapter 16

The doctor is often more to be feared than the disease. ~ Voltaire

In the sleek, ultramodern office of Dr. Drusen, the world-renowned retinal specialist referred by Dr. Glaukomflecken, Cunegonde and the Old Woman once again found themselves navigating the complex world of eye care.

The office was defined by its sleek lines and shiny surfaces, with every angle meticulously crafted. Natural light cascaded gently through the expansive, floor-to-ceiling windows, bathing the room in a warm, golden glow. The walls displayed large, framed certificates proclaiming Dr. Drusen's extensive credentials, interspersed with abstract paintings of the human eye in vivid colors. Tucked away in a corner, a small plaque read, "Owned and operated by Shylock Capital: Pound of Flesh Investments by Don Issachar Private Equity LLC."

Dr. Drusen, known for his meticulous work and a name that seemed to affirm the retinal heritage in his DNA, greeted them with a reassuring smile. Tall and lean, he stood with a posture ramrod straight. His hair, a glossy sheen of silver, was meticulously combed back to reveal a high forehead. His round glasses, with lenses so thick, made his eyes appear as pinpoints.

"Ah, Cunegonde and dear Old Woman," Dr. Drusen began, extending a warm handshake. "I've heard much about your ocular adventures. Dr. Glaukomflecken has briefed me thoroughly on your situation. A case of retinal detachment, is it? How very . . . well, *detached* of them."

Cunegonde replied, "Yes, they've decided to go AWOL, it seems. We were hoping you might persuade them to report back to duty."

The Old Woman, peering at the doctor through her troubled eyes, added, "And preferably sooner rather than later. My world's become quite blurry."

Dr. Drusen chuckled. "Fear not, for I am a master of retinal reattachment. I'll have your retinas back in place before you can say *macular degeneration.* It's all in a day's work for Dr. Drusen."

Cunegonde quipped, "Let's hope your hands are as skilled as your humor is sharp."

"Ah," Dr. Drusen replied, "humor is but a small part of my repertoire. My real talent lies in convincing wayward retinas to return to their rightful places. Consider me a retina wrangler, if you will."

The Old Woman, intrigued, asked, "And should we prepare any offerings or sacrifices to aid in their reattachment?"

Dr. Drusen, amused, replied, "No sacrifices necessary. No, all we need is precision, skill, and perhaps a little bit of retinal charm."

Cunegonde, growing impatient, blurted out, "Dr. Drusen, please cut to the chase. What are the surgical options for my dear friend, the Old Woman?"

"Ah, my esteemed patient," Dr. Drusen began, rubbing his hands together with the glee of a child in a candy store. "We stand at the forefront of modern ophthalmology, where cutting-edge science meets the delicate art of retinal reattachment. Allow me to introduce you to the range of options at our disposal."

Cunegonde, leaned in with interest. "Do tell, Dr. Drusen," she said. "We're all ears."

"First of all," Dr. Drusen started, "we have the scleral buckle. Think of it as a belt for the eye, cinching everything back into place. It's vintage, it's classic."

The Old Woman chimed in, "Will this belt come in leather or canvas?"

Dr. Drusen chuckled. "Ah, we opt for a more eye-friendly material like silicone. Moving on, we have the vitrectomy, a procedure that's as fun to say as it is to perform. We remove the vitreous gel, clear out any debris, and help your retina return to its original position."

Cunegonde raised an eyebrow. "Sounds like a spring cleaning for the eye."

Dr. Drusen replied with a grin, "Exactly. Next, we have laser treatment, a precise and elegant solution. It's like using a lightsaber to reattach the retina—very chic indeed."

The Old Woman pondered a moment, then responded with a twinkle in her eye, "I always fancied myself as a bit of a Jedi."

Dr. Drusen continued, "Then, we have the option of using gas or silicone oil to fill the eye and push the retina back into place. Think of it like choosing between two fine wines, each with its own unique bouquet and finish."

"I suppose we'll go with the vintage that pairs best with ocular health," Cunegonde commented with a wry smile.

Dr. Drusen turned serious. "Finally, regardless of the choice, our goal is clear: to reattach the retina with the finesse of a master chef plating a Michelin-star dish."

The Old Woman, enjoying the doctor's extended metaphor, smiled. "Well, Dr. Drusen, as long as I don't end up on the menu, I'm ready to place my order. Let's opt for the treatment that promises a feast for the eyes."

Cunegonde, amused by the repartee, turned towards Dr. Drusen, inquiring, "So, Dr. Drusen, which dish do you recommend for our dear Old Woman? Which treatment is truly the *crème de la crème?*"

"Ah," he began, pausing thoughtfully, "choosing the right procedure is akin to selecting the perfect wine for dinner. It's not merely about what's universally best but what's best for the individual palate—or in this case, the eye. Each treatment option has its merits, but it must align perfectly with the patient's specific condition and needs."

The Old Woman added, "Well, I do fancy myself a bit of a sommelier when it comes to surgeries. Something with a full body, a hint of lasers, perhaps, with a smooth, retinal finish?"

Dr. Drusen chuckled. "Given the specific vintage of your retinal detachment, I would recommend the scleral buckle. It's traditional, yet effective—a true classic. Like a fine Bordeaux, it has stood the test of time and complements most conditions wonderfully."

"And what of the side dishes? Any laser garnishing or gas infusion to complete the meal?" Cunegonde asked.

"Ah, the laser treatment could indeed serve as an exquisite garnish," Dr. Drusen replied, "enhancing the main course by ensuring the retina stays in place, much like a sprinkle of parsley over the entrée for that extra touch of elegance."

The Old Woman, queried, "And the recovery period? Should we expect a full-bodied experience, or more of a light, airy sensation?"

"Think of it as savoring a fine wine," Dr. Drusen advised. "Initially, there might be a robust, somewhat intense flavor—some discomfort and the need for rest. But, given time, it will mellow into a pleasant, satisfying finish, with the clarity of vision restored much like the palate after a delightful meal."

Cunegonde nodded. "Well, as long as we're dining in the Michelin-starred section of surgeries, I suppose we're in good hands. Chef Drusen, we'll have what you're recommending."

Dr. Drusen, delighted with their decision, assured them, "Excellent choice. I'll ensure that the Old Woman's eyes receive the culinary masterpiece they deserve. We'll have her feasting on the full smorgasbord of sight in no time."

The Old Woman leaned in, her curiosity piqued by a sudden thought. "Dr. Drusen," she began, "if I were your mother, which procedure would you choose for me? Would you still recommend the scleral buckle, or is there a secret family recipe you've been holding out on us?"

"Ah," he said, "if you were my mother, I suppose I would have to consider not just the efficacy of the treatment but also the comfort and recovery time. After all, family dinners might never be the same if I chose poorly."

Cunegonde leaned forward. "Yes, do tell. Is there a VIP treatment in the retinal world? A gold-plated scleral buckle, perhaps?"

Dr. Drusen smiled. "For my mother—or you, in this endearing hypothetical—I would still recommend the scleral buckle. It's tried and true, much like a cherished family recipe that has been passed down through generations. However, I'd enhance it with a dash of laser photocoagulation, to ensure the retina stays firmly in place."

The Old Woman nodded. "I see," she quipped, "no pun intended."

"None taken," Dr. Drusen replied, laughing. "And rest assured—the post-operative care would be akin to the tender, loving care one reserves for family members. You'd be under strict instructions to enjoy copious amounts of rest, perhaps with a side of your favorite television programs, all served on a comfortable recliner."

Cunegonde, smiling, added, "Sounds like the recovery period might be more enjoyable than a family reunion. Less drama, more Netflix."

"Exactly," Dr. Drusen agreed. "And I'd be calling to check in, not just as your surgeon, but as an honorary family member concerned about the well-being of his dear *mother*."

The Old Woman, chuckling, concluded, "Well then, Dr. Drusen, I suppose I'm ready to be adopted into your illustrious family of retinal success stories. So, when's dinner?"

With that, they all shared a lighthearted laugh. They parted ways with smiles; the Old Woman felt like a member of Dr. Drusen's extended medical family, ready to face her surgery with a newfound sense of confidence and camaraderie.

After the grand spectacle of retinal surgery—a veritable buffet of scleral buckle, vitrectomy, laser, and gas, all meticulously prepared and served by Dr. Drusen himself—the Old Woman found herself back in the sleek shiny consultation room the day after the operation. The surgery, while a marvel of modern medicine, had left her vision as murky as looking through frosted glass smeared with petroleum gel.

"So, Dr. Drusen," the Old Woman began, her tone light despite the gravity of the situation. "It seems my eyes have decided to remain in the impressionist period, despite your best efforts to bring them into high-definition reality. Though I must say, the retinas seem to have returned home, firmly attached."

Dr. Drusen, leaning back in his chair, stroked his chin. "Indeed, the retinas are back where they belong, courtesy of the scleral buckle, laser, and gas—a testament to the exquisite symphony of procedures I orchestrated. However, it seems your corneas have thrown us a curveball, swelling—presumably with pride—from participating in such a groundbreaking surgical endeavor."

Cunegonde, cut in, "Or perhaps they're simply swelling with confusion."

Dr. Drusen nodded. "A fair assessment. The corneas are indeed like the uninvited guests to our vision party, reacting, shall we say, a tad dramatically. But fear not, for I propose a period of observation—two weeks of observing and waiting, as if we're binge-watching the drama of healing unfold—*Let the Swelling Subside!*"

The Old Woman sighed. "Ah, more waiting. I was hoping for a grand reveal, not a cliffhanger. Still, if my eyes are the main characters in this drama, I suppose we must give them time to develop."

"Yes," Dr. Drusen agreed, "consider this the intermission of our play, a brief pause for refreshments and anticipation-building before the grand finale. And in this case, the refreshments are a healthy dose of patience, with a side of cautious optimism."

Cunegonde, raising an eyebrow, shot back, "Well, as long as the final act doesn't involve more surprises. My nerves can only handle so much suspense."

"Understood," Dr. Drusen replied with a smile. "We'll aim for a resolution that satisfies our audience—no plot twists, just a smooth transition to a clear, sharp denouement."

The Old Woman, attempting to peer at the doctor through her foggy vision, quipped, "I'll hold you to that, Dr. Drusen. And perhaps, once this is all over, we can consider a sequel. Something with less drama and more comedy, I hope."

"As do I," Dr. Drusen concurred. "As do I."

#

Two weeks passed—a fortnight of anticipation, during which the Old Woman's eyes had been stewing in their own little atmospheric bubble, courtesy of Dr. Drusen's surgical smorgasbord, as they found themselves once again in the familiar confines of Dr. Drusen's office.

"Dr. Drusen," the Old Woman began, her voice exasperated, "my vision is no better than two weeks ago. Plus, I've been feeling rather light-headed."

"Ah, it's the helium bubbles that were placed in your eyes to keep your retinas in their proper place," Dr. Drusen replied, ever the picture of composure. "Yes, an unusual side effect, to be sure. It's not every day one can say their buoyancy is due to their ocular enhancements. Consider it a temporary lift in spirit, if you will."

Raising one eyebrow, Cunegonde interjected, "Are we sure she won't just float away one of these days?"

Dr. Drusen nodded, his composure ever intact. "A prudent measure, but I assure you, the helium's effects are strictly metaphorical. As for the corneas, they remain swollen."

The Old Woman, leaning forward, squinted, struggling to see Dr. Drusen close up. "So, what's the plan? More waiting? "

"Patience, my dear," Dr. Drusen advised, his tone gentle yet firm. "Your eyes are composing a symphony, and every note must be played in its own time. We'll reconvene in a month, giving the corneas a chance to deflate their egos and the helium gas to make its grand exit."

Cunegonde responded with a sigh. "At this rate, we'll have enough material for a trilogy—*The Old Woman's Eyes: A Tale of Gas, Buoyancy, and Swollen Pride.*"

Dr. Drusen smiled. "A New York Times Bestseller, no less. And I, your humble first-person narrator, shall guide us to a resolution worthy of such an epic saga."

The Old Woman, attempting to muster a smile through her frustration, concluded, "Well, Dr. Drusen, I do hope the next chapter involves less gas and more clarity."

#

One month later, in the now all-too-familiar surroundings of Dr. Drusen's office, the Old Woman and Cunegonde made their grand re-entrance. The helium saga had come to a close, much to the relief of all involved. However, the victory was bittersweet, as her vision had not only failed to improve but had in fact worsened.

"Dr. Drusen," the Old Woman began, her tone resigned, "now my world looks like peering through a frosted glass window smeared with peanut butter. On the bright side, my lightheadedness has resolved. I suppose I should be grateful for small mercies."

Dr. Drusen, standing with the air of a general who had won a hard-fought battle, nodded solemnly. "Indeed, the helium has lifted, and your retinas remain steadfastly in place, a testament to our efforts. However, it seems your corneas have joined the rebellion, swelling—perhaps out of envy for the attention your retinas have received, or maybe in a bid to star in their own dramatic saga."

Cunegonde interposed, "So, what's the next step? Is there a specialist for rebellious corneas?"

Dr. Drusen announced, "Ah, for that, we turn to the illustrious Dr. Guttata, a virtuoso in the realm of corneal conundrums.

His expertise in taming the tempestuous tides of corneal swelling is unparalleled. I have reattached the retinas, my chapter in this saga is complete. Dr. Guttata will pick up the quill and pen the next chapter."

The Old Woman quipped, "From retinal reattachments to corneal calamities, my eyes are certainly getting a comprehensive tour of the world of ophthalmology. Do you suppose Dr. Guttata enjoys a good helium joke?"

"Dr. Guttata is renowned not only for his skill but also for his impeccable bedside manner and sense of humor," Dr. Drusen replied. "I dare say, he might find the story of your buoyant interlude uplifting."

Cunegonde, with a wry smile, said, "Well, as long as he refrains from filling my dear Old Woman's eyes with more gas, we might just get along. We've certainly had our fill of gaseous grandstanding for one lifetime."

Dr. Drusen chuckled. "Fear not, dear Old Woman, Dr. Guttata's treatments are firmly grounded in reality. No more flights of fancy for your eyes, I assure you."

Chapter 17

Paradise is where I am. ~ Voltaire

The trio, Candide, Cacambo, and Pangloss awoke the next morning feeling refreshed and eager to explore more of Eldorado's splendors. As promised, the Eldoradian guide arrived to escort them to their royal audience.

"Good morning, esteemed guests! I trust you found your accommodation satisfactory?" he inquired politely.

"Oh, more than satisfactory!" Candide exclaimed. "I haven't slept that soundly in ages. Eldorado's beds put even the finest inns to shame."

Pangloss nodded. "Quite right, quite right! Why, I feel reinvigorated and ready to soak in more of your marvelous city."

Cacambo, stretching his arms, just waking up, added with a yawn, "And I must agree; it's as if these beds are blessed by the gods themselves."

"Excellent!" The guide said. "If you'll follow me, it's time to present you to His Majesty, our king."

As they continued through the city, Candide could not peel his eyes away from the magnificent structures around them. The buildings towered impossibly high, with soaring pillars and arched windows that let in ample sunlight. Intricate carvings and mosaics adorned every surface.

But most astonishing was an enormous aqueduct spanning between two massive towers. Crystal clear water flowed swiftly up through its center, defying gravity.

"Remarkable!" Candide exclaimed. "It seems you've conquered even gravity itself."

Their guide chuckled. "Our engineers are quite skilled in manipulating the natural forces through ingenious techniques. But you'll see even greater wonders soon enough."

At last, they arrived at the royal palace, an imposing structure of white marble and gold filigree. The soaring spires gleamed in the morning light.

Candide and Cacambo gaped upwards, necks craning to take in the towering marble edifice studded with gold and gems that gleamed in the morning sun. Intricately carved statues of ancient kings and heroes adorned the entrance, and a long crimson carpet marked their path inside. They passed through the massive doors into the throne room. Gilded columns lined the hall, stretching toward the vaulted ceilings adorned with colorful frescoes. The floors, polished marble, were complemented by plush rugs woven in vibrant hues.

At the top of a small flight of steps sat an imposing, regal figure draped in luxurious purple and gold robes. Atop his head glittered a crown encrusted with diamonds and other precious gems. His countenance was as noble as the ancient statues lining Eldorado's grand avenues. His eyes sparked a lively curiosity, an eternal youthfulness that spoke of a heart unhardened by time. His hair was a magnificent mane of silver waves flowing back from his highbrow, each strand catching and reflecting a different shade of the morning's light.

"Greetings, visitors," his voice resonated through the hall, both commanding and gracious. "I am the king of Eldorado. Welcome to my kingdom."

Candide, Pangloss, and Cacambo hastily prostrated themselves on the gleaming marble floor before the king's throne. "You honor us beyond measure with your hospitality, Your Majesty," Candide said, voice echoing in the cavernous throne room. "We did not expect to stumble upon a realm as wondrous as Eldorado."

He heard soft footsteps as the king descended the steps towards them. "Please rise, my friends," the king gently bid them. "Here in Eldorado, we are all equals. A simple bow will suffice."

Candide slowly stood, raising his eyes once more to the king's kind yet regal countenance.

"I am but a humble wanderer who arrived here by chance," Candide demurred, still awestruck by the posh opulence of the throne room. "To be welcomed so warmly is more than I could have imagined."

The king smiled, eyes crinkling with mirth. "And yet providence saw fit to guide you here, to our hidden sanctuary," he replied. "Come, be at ease. Tonight, you shall dine at my table as honored guests."

Candide bowed deeply once more. "Your kindness knows no bounds, Your Majesty. After our long and arduous journey, your offer of hospitality is most welcome."

"We are most grateful, Your Majesty," Pangloss added. "Indeed, the existence of such a place as Eldorado proves the world has much hidden goodness."

The king beckoned them forward into an even more lavish room. "Come, my new friends, sit and take your ease."

Servants brought trays laden with refreshments and exotic fruits the likes of which Candide had never seen. His stomach rumbled despite himself. After days of privation, the sight of such bounty was overwhelming.

Beside him, Pangloss's eyes shone with curiosity as he surveyed their lavish surroundings. "Your Majesty, I am eager to uncover the secret behind Eldorado's remarkable prosperity. How have you managed to forge such an equitable and harmonious society?"

The king smiled with benevolence. "The answer is simple, my friend. Here in Eldorado, our equity is rooted in the fundamental belief that every human life is invaluable—no one's station in life is above or below anyone else's."

"As for harmony," he continued, "from a very young age, every Eldoradian is taught to devote themselves to the community, just as Eldorado commits to the well-being of each of its citizens. Here, no one goes hungry or remains uncared for."

Pangloss nodded. "Ah, truly a utopia where *equity and inclusion* are not mere ideals, but the very foundations of society. What profound lessons the rest of the world could learn from Eldorado!"

As the afternoon unfolded amidst a haze of food and wine, the king and Pangloss delved into a spirited discussion on philosophy and governance. Meanwhile, Candide sat back, letting the warmth and comfort of Eldorado wash over him. For the moment, he desired nothing more. Gazing out at the lush paradise surrounding the palace, he marveled at the seamless blend of harmony and prosperity that set Eldorado apart from the strife and misery he had known since leaving Boston.

"Pardon my interruption, Your Majesty," Candide interjected, curiosity in his voice. "I must inquire—what is the secret behind Eldorado's abundant wealth? How have you cultivated such a perfect society?"

The king regarded Candide thoughtfully before replying, "It's straightforward, my friend. Among us, wealth is not measured by material possessions, but by the appreciation of wisdom, imagination, and the intrinsic value of human life."

Candide's eyes widened with interest. "Please, elaborate," he implored.

"Our greatest wealth lies within our people—the diversity of their abilities, skills, and talents enriches us all," the king proclaimed. "We hold the arts, sciences, and innovations in high regard, nurturing each citizen's potential through comprehensive education and a supportive community. As a result, Eldorado has flourished, sustained by the remarkable contributions of its citizens across generations."

Pangloss beamed in appreciation. "A wise and enlightened approach indeed! It seems, in Eldorado, you have realized the zenith of civilization through *diversity, equity, and inclusion!*"

But Candide still looked puzzled. "Forgive me, Your Majesty, but how were such ideals practically implemented? What policies or laws enabled this societal structure?"

The king laughed gently. "No policies or laws, merely principles seamlessly woven into our social fabric. When all are united by shared values, the need for enforcement dissolves."

Pangloss rubbed his chin, his curiosity heightened. "Intriguing! But what of governance? How is order maintained in your society without formal institutions?"

The king's eyes crinkled. "Through mutual understanding and respect, my friends. Here in Eldorado, all citizens collaborate for the common good. Coercion is unnecessary when people naturally act with concern for their neighbors."

Cacambo, who had been quietly surveying his surroundings and partaking in the sumptuous fare, leaned in closer. "But surely, Your Majesty," he interjected with a hint of skepticism in his voice. "There must be challenges that arise even in such a paradise."

The king's expression turned contemplative. "Indeed," he conceded, "perfection is an ideal we strive for rather than a constant state. We, too, face our trials and tribulations. However, we resolve them through counsel and understanding rather than conflict."

"And what of those who dissent?" Candide asked, his curiosity piqued by the implication that not all was as perfect as it appeared.

The king sipped from a goblet adorned with jewels before responding. "Dissent is natural in any society," he began, "for without the freedom to question and debate, wisdom cannot flourish. Those who disagree with our ways are given a voice and platform to speak their minds. Our scholars and legislators then discuss these matters, always seeking a resolution that benefits the greater good. If no consensus can be reached, we agree to respect our differences, as long as they cause no harm to others."

Cacambo nodded thoughtfully. "A fair and just approach, it seems. And if someone were to wish to leave Eldorado?"

The king's eyes held a touch of sadness. "It is rare, but it happens. We do not hold anyone against their will; the pursuit of happiness is an individual journey. Should one of our citizens wish to depart for the outside world, they are free to do so—with the understanding that they can never return, for the way to Eldorado must remain a secret."

"Then how did we manage to find ourselves in Eldorado?" Candide asked.

The king leaned back in his seat, a playful gleam in his eyes. "Ah, you see, not all who wander are lost, and not all paths to Eldorado are closed forever. Sometimes, the land itself seems to call out to certain souls, drawing them to its borders. This is a rare occurrence, of course—a confluence of fateful events and pure chance. You have experienced what few ever will. You are welcome to stay in Eldorado for as long as you wish."

Pangloss conjectured, "It seems Eldorado is organic. It selects its inhabitants."

The king responded, "In a way, yes. It is not so much selection as it is attraction. Our paradise exists in harmony with the Universe, and at times, that harmony extends its reach to those who seek or need it most. Eldorado's very essence is bound to the cosmic equilibrium—like a note in an eternal symphony, attracting those attuned to its music."

As the evening light waned and gave way to the Milky Way, the conversation around the king's table grew more intimate and philosophical. Candide watched as the servants lit lanterns that cast a golden glow over the faces of his companions.

"Your Majesty," Candide ventured, his voice tinged with a newfound hope, "if Eldorado is so rich in virtue and happiness, could its principles not be spread to the world beyond? Could others not benefit from your enlightened approach?"

The king's expression grew somber; he paused before answering. "Candide, my dear friend, what you propose is a noble idea. But one must understand that our way of life is the fruit of this particular soil; it has grown from our unique circumstances and history. To transplant it elsewhere would require more than mere teachings—it would need a fertile ground in which similar values are already sprouting."

Pangloss nodded at the king's words. "Indeed, Your Majesty," he concurred, "for Voltaire himself said that *the best of all possible worlds is a matter of philosophical debate, not geographical transplantation.* The glorious nature of Eldorado might very well wither in a soil not prepared for its growth."

As the night deepened, the talk shifted from philosophy to stories of Eldorado's past. The king recounted tales of ancient wisdom preserved through generations and legendary heroes who had shaped their society with acts of valor and kindness. Each story wove a thread into the rich tapestry of their culture and history, embodying the principles that made their society thrive.

Candide listened with rapt attention, each tale a testament to the wonders of this hidden utopia. After a pregnant pause, he leaned forward earnestly. "Your Majesty," he began, shifting the subject, "you have shared much about your culture, justice system, and history. But what about the well-being of your citizens? How do they maintain such good health? Wherever I go, I see people who are strong, and their vitality never seems to diminish with age."

The king replied, "Much of our health and longevity are due to the tranquil atmosphere and the cooperative spirit in Eldorado. However, we Eldoradians changed for the better in our health many eons ago when one of ancient healers discovered the Regenfruit Tree."

The king's gaze turned distant as he recounted the legend of the Regenfruit Tree, his voice resonating like an echo from the ancient times of Eldorado.

In the heart of Eldorado, nestled amidst lush greenery and shimmering streams, there grew a plant unlike any other—the Regenfruit Tree. Its branches bowed beneath the weight of plump, golden fruits.

The Regenfruit Tree traces its lineage to the dawn of Eldorado itself. According to ancient lore, it was a gift from the gods, bestowed upon the land to grant its inhabitants the power of regeneration—the ability to heal and restore what had been lost.

The fruit of the Regenfruit Tree was a true elixir of life, capable of awakening dormant stem cells and initiating a remarkable journey of regeneration. Upon consumption, its sweet nectar flowed through the vessels, infusing each cell with vitality and vigor, and igniting a spark of renewal from within.

Among the citizens of Eldorado, the Regenfruit Tree stood as a revered symbol of hope and resilience—a beacon of light in their darkest times. In moments of sickness or injury, they sought solace from the tree, plucking its fruits with deep reverence and gratitude. Each succulent bite was cherished, carrying with it the promise of healing and restoration.

One such tale spoke of a young maiden, named Lysandra, whose eyes had been robbed of sight by a cruel twist of fate. Desperate to reclaim the world she had lost, Lysandra embarked on a pilgrimage to the sacred grove where the Regenfruit Tree stood sentinel.

She plucked a ripe fruit from the boughs above, its golden hue gleaming in the dappled sunlight. Closing her eyes, she bit into the fruit, savoring its sweetness as it filled her senses. In the days that followed, a miracle unfolded before the eyes of the Eldoradians. Where once darkness had reigned, light now danced like a symphony of colors. Lysandra's sight was restored, her eyes alighted with wonder and gratitude as she beheld the world anew.

Lysandra then went forth to spread the healing power of Regenfruit Tree to all of Eldorado. From every corner of Eldorado, the sick and suffering— be they lame, deaf, blind, mute, deformed, demented—made their pilgrimage to the grove where the Regenfruit grew. Soon news of miraculous cures spread far and wide. From that day forth, the Regenfruit Tree became more than a mere plant—it was a testament to the resilience of the human spirit, a reminder that even in the face of adversity, there existed the power to heal, to grow, and to thrive.

And so, the legend of the Regenfruit Tree lived on, its branches reaching ever skyward, its fruits a source of hope and inspiration for generations to come. In the verdant paradise of Eldorado, the miracle of regeneration bloomed eternal, nourished by the timeless wisdom of the land and the boundless compassion of its people.

Later in the evening, relaxing in the plush cushions of their luxurious quarters, Candide replayed the day's events in his mind—the audience with the benevolent king, the lavish feast, the enlightening conversations with the Eldoradians about their harmonious society, and the Regenfruit tree. It seemed a dream compared to the hardships he had endured prior to arriving here.

"Well, Pangloss," he remarked, "it appears your optimism was not entirely misplaced after all. This land seems to be a living embodiment of your philosophy that we inhabit the *best of all possible worlds.*"

Pangloss chuckled, sipping Eldoradian wine from a jewel-encrusted goblet. "I must admit, even I did not anticipate stumbling upon such an idyllic society! But it just goes to show, my dear Candide, that there is always a method to the madness of life's twists and turns."

Nearby, Cacambo was carefully polishing a golden statue he had been gifted. "I hope you two aren't thinking of leaving anytime soon," he said. "I could get used to this sort of treatment. No pesky adventures, just lying in the lap of luxury!"

Candide laughed. "Not to worry, my friend. I think we have all earned a respite from peril. Let us enjoy Eldorado's hospitality a while longer before we contemplate our next journey."

Chapter 18

The art of medicine consists of amusing the patient
while nature cures the disease. ~ Voltaire

Cunegonde and the Old Woman entered Dr. Guttata's office, a space that radiated an air of serene confidence, much like the doctor himself. Known far and wide as a pioneer in corneal transplantation, Dr. Guttata's reputation preceded him.

The office was decorated with a tasteful minimalism, the walls adorned with framed certificates and accolades attesting to Dr. Guttata's accomplishments. A large window allowed gentle streams of sunlight to dance across the polished wooden floor, endowing the space with a warm, inviting glow. A small plaque, placed below the frames read, "Owned and operated by Gold Coin Consortium: Profiting from Misfortune with Don Issachar Private Equity LLC."

Dr Guttata was a man of an undefinable age, between youthful exuberance and distinguished maturity, with a head of flaming red hair that defied gravity. Each individual strand appeared to have been coaxed by an unseen force into an upward swirl. His eyes were two sparkling sapphires, set deep within their sockets. His nose, noble and aquiline, was offset by a mustache, trimmed using the golden ratio—a masterpiece of facial topiary!

"Dr. Guttata," Cunegonde began, "after a grand adventure with retinal detachments and helium-filled eyes, we find ourselves at your doorstep, seeking guidance for the Old Woman's swollen corneas. We've heard you're the Magellan of the corneal world."

Dr. Guttata, with a smile, replied, "I'm flattered by the comparison, though I assure you, my explorations tend to be far less treacherous than Magellan's. Tell me about your journey thus far."

The Old Woman, with effort, fashioned the best eyeroll she could, then sighed before recounting their odyssey, from the helium highs to the swollen sorrows. "And so," she concluded, "we arrive, hoping you might chart a course through these murky waters."

"Ah," Dr. Guttata said, leaning back thoughtfully. "Remember the eyes are *windows to the soul!* They are indeed a frontier of their own, fraught with mysteries and marvels. Your corneas, swollen as they are, signal their distress, much like a lighthouse warns ships of perilous shores."

Cunegonde asked, "And do you have a map for these perilous shores, Dr. Guttata? A way to calm the stormy seas of her corneas?"

Dr. Guttata nodded. "Indeed, I do. Considering the saga you've both endured, I believe a corneal transplantation, or what we call a keratoplasty, might be the beacon of hope we're looking for. It's a procedure where we replace the troubled corneal tissue with a clear, healthy one, much like replacing a fogged window with one that offers a clear view."

The Old Woman, intrigued yet apprehensive, queried, "And is this transplantation an epic of its own? Should we brace for more adventures?"

"With every great tale comes its challenges," Dr. Guttata admitted, "but fear not. I've navigated these waters many a time, and while the journey requires care and patience, the destination—a clear vision—is well worth the voyage."

Cunegonde added, "As long as there are no helium balloons involved, Dr. Guttata, we place our trust in your compass and your skills."

Dr. Guttata assured them, "I'll ensure your journey is as smooth as possible. With a bit of modern medical magic and a dash of patience, we'll aim for a horizon where the Old Woman can see the world anew, not as a frosted glass painting, but with the clarity and beauty it possesses."

Cunegonde and the Old Woman, now seasoned veterans of the ophthalmic odyssey, sat enthralled before Dr. Guttata. The world of corneal transplantation lay before them, a new chapter in their saga, ripe with possibilities and, inevitably, more medical acronyms.

"Dr. Guttata," Cunegonde began, her voice carrying a hint of confusion, "we've come across terms like PK, DSEK, and DMEK. It sounds like we're choosing between spy agencies rather than surgical options. Could you enlighten us on these covert operations?"

Amused, Dr. Guttata answered, "Ah, yes, the world of corneal transplantation is indeed filled with acronyms that could rival any secret service. Let's demystify these options, shall we?"

"First, we have Penetrating Keratoplasty, or PK," he continued in earnest, "a full-thickness transplant. Think of it as a wholesale renovation, where we replace the entire window rather than just patching up the cracks. It's the most comprehensive makeover your eye could hope for."

The Old Woman, nodding along, interjected, "So, PK is like hiring an interior designer for a complete overhaul. Does it come with new curtains?"

"Metaphorically speaking, yes," Dr. Guttata chuckled. "Then there's DSEK, Descemet's Stripping Endothelial Keratoplasty, where we replace only the inner layers of the cornea. It's akin to re-finishing the floors of your home without tearing down the walls."

Cunegonde quipped, "A less invasive home improvement, then. And what of DMEK? Does that involve knocking down any metaphorical walls?"

"DMEK, or Descemet Membrane Endothelial Keratoplasty, is even more precise," Dr. Guttata explained. "In this procedure, we replace only the very innermost layer—the Descemet membrane and endothelium. Think of it like changing the wallpaper in a room; it completely transforms the appearance without altering the underlying structure."

The Old Woman mused, "Fascinating. So, we're deciding between a full house renovation, refinishing the floors, or simply changing the wallpaper. And here I thought I was just here to fix my eyes, not redecorate."

Dr. Guttata concluded, "Exactly. Each option has its own benefits and is suitable for different conditions. Rest assured, we'll select the procedure that best fits the unique architecture of your eyes. We aim for a restoration that not only looks aesthetically pleasing but also enhances your vision, ensuring the interior matches the beautiful exterior."

Leaning back, Cunegonde tried to wrap things up with a hint of reservation. "Well, Dr. Guttata, it seems we're in good hands, whether we're opting for a full renovation or just a minor touch-up. Just promise us there's no DIY involved. We've all seen how those projects turn out on reality TV."

Dr. Guttata assured, "No DIY, I promise. Only the finest craftsmanship for our dear Old Woman's eyes."

Cunegonde felt the need to explain what they'd already been through. "Dr. Guttata, given the myriad of options from the full-thickness extravaganza to the minimalist wallpaper approach, which do you reckon is our golden ticket? We're hoping for a grand reveal that doesn't end with, *And behind door number three is . . . more surgery*, since we've had several priors to this.'"

Dr. Guttata leaned forward. "Ah, if only the choice came with a sparkling game show host. Given the state of the Old Woman's corneas, swollen as they are from their recent adventures, and considering the grand odyssey you've both embarked upon, I'm inclined to recommend the DMEK procedure."

Looking at both women, he paused, then continued, "It's true, this is the most delicate option; it offers a refined touch, akin to a master painter applying the final strokes to a masterpiece. The recovery is generally quicker, and the visual outcomes can be quite spectacular. Plus, I assure you, it comes with the added benefit of no helium involvement."

"So, DMEK is our path to enlightenment," said The Old Woman, " . . . or at least to better sight. It sounds almost as if we're opting for a spiritual journey, not just a surgical one."

Cunegonde nodded. "Well, as long as this path doesn't lead us to *The Twilight Zone* of endless surgeries, I'm all for it. How soon can we embark on this *final stroke of the master painter?*"

Dr. Guttata assured them he would schedule the procedure as soon as they gave him the go-ahead. "Consider it less a journey into *The Twilight Zone* and more a voyage back to the vivid colors and clear lines of reality," he told them. "I'll be your guide, ensuring the path is smooth and the outcome, I hope, worthy of a prime-time reveal."

The Old Woman declared, "Then let us proceed. Onward to clarity, away from the land of shadows and into the light. Or, at the very least, into a world where I can read the fine print without summoning a microscope."

As the consultation with Dr. Guttata was drawing to a close, the Old Woman leaned in, ready to pose a question that had become somewhat of a tradition in their medical journey. "Dr. Guttata," she said, her voice laced with a blend of curiosity, "if I were your mother, navigating through this maze of corneal conundrums, which procedure would you choose for me? Would you still suggest the DMEK, or is there a secret, family-only recipe for clear vision that you've been holding out on us?"

Dr. Guttata's face broke into a grin. "Ah, if you were *my mother*," he mused, tapping his chin thoughtfully, "I suppose I would have to consider not only the best clinical outcome but also the comfort and recovery process. After all, a son's duty is to ensure his mother's journey is as smooth as possible."

"For my mother, I would indeed recommend the DMEK procedure. It's akin to gifting her a pair of the finest silk gloves instead of rugged work gloves. Both protect the hands, but the silk gloves do so with a gentleness and finesse that's unparalleled."

Cunegonde quipped, "Silk gloves, you say? Here I was, thinking we were in the business of eye surgery, not accessorizing for a gala."

Dr. Guttata laughed. "Well, Cunegonde, in the world of corneal surgery, DMEK is as close to the elegance of a gala as we get. It offers clarity and recovery fit for a queen—or in this case, my mother, ensuring she returns to her royal duties."

The Old Woman chirped, "Well, then, Dr. Guttata, let's proceed with the DMEK. If it's good enough for your hypothetical mother, it's certainly royal enough for me."

Dr. Guttata replied, "We'll treat you with the care and respect befitting royalty, ensuring your coronation—ah, I mean, your surgery—is a crowning success."

#

The day after the DMEK surgery, the Old Woman and Cunegonde found themselves once again in the familiar, albeit now almost familial, setting of Dr. Guttata's office. Despite the successful attachment of the corneal transplants, the world through the Old Woman's eyes was as clear as looking through a shattered glass.

"Dr. Guttata," the Old Woman exasperated, "it seems my eyes have decided to celebrate the surgery by inflating themselves like balloons at a birthday party. And here I thought we were done with air-filled adventures."

Dr. Guttata, ever the embodiment of calm and confidence, replied with a gentle chuckle. "Ah, the post-operative air. Consider it a temporary cushion, ensuring the transplants remain exactly where they should. Though, I admit, the pressure did rise a bit more than we'd like—perhaps a bit too enthusiastic in its protective role, a bit too bloated in its vigilance. I'll need to let some air out of the eyes."

Cunegonde inquired about the solution. "I'm imagining a tiny valve on the side of her eye now. Should we expect a hissing sound? Or would it be more akin to a flatus?"

With a smile, Dr. Guttata explained, "The process is a bit more sophisticated than deflating a balloon or passing gas, but the principle is similar. By carefully adjusting the pressure, we ensure the eye returns to a more comfortable state. No hissing sound or farting required, though that would make for an interesting party trick."

The Old Woman quipped, "My mother always said—it's better out than in. Please let us get on with it."

Dr Guttata proceeded to let some air out of the Old Woman's eyes. True to his words, the procedure was accompanied by neither hissing sounds nor flatulence, only the quiet concentration of an artist at work. As the pressure within her eyes gently reduced, the Old Woman felt a subtle easing, a hint that the world might soon come back into focus.

Afterwards, Dr. Guttata assured the Old Woman, "Rest assured, your eyes will remain firmly grounded. The surgery was a success, and the transplants are perfectly positioned. Now, it's a matter of patience as your eyes adjust and the remaining air dissipates naturally. Your vision will clear up in time, much like a fog lifting at dawn."

Cunegonde added, her voice tinged with resignation, "So, we're dawn chasers now, waiting for the fog to lift. I'll make sure to wake the Old Woman up at sunrise; perhaps it'll speed up the process."

"A sunrise vigil sounds like a splendid idea," the good doctor replied, his tone encouraging, "though not strictly necessary. I'll see you both in two weeks, and by then, I expect we'll be seeing significant improvements."

#

Two weeks had passed since the air-filled escapade, and Cunegonde and the Old Woman showed up once again to the calming presence of Dr. Guttata. The Old Woman's eyes were no longer the swollen spectacles they once were, thanks to the corneal transplants. However, the celebration was tempered by the persistence of high eye pressure and a vision that was still as blurry as a Monet painting viewed at arm's length.

"Dr. Guttata," Cunegonde said with concern, "While we're thrilled to bid adieu to the corneal swelling—truly, it's been an adventure—I can't help but notice we've traded one issue for another.

The eye pressures? Still a high-flier. And her vision? Let's just say, she won't be spotting needles in haystacks anytime soon."

Dr. Guttata nodded, commiserating. "Indeed, the corneal transplants have settled beautifully, a tribute to the resilience of the Old Woman's eyes. However, the saga of her vision continues, with glaucoma now taking center stage. It seems the torch must be passed once again."

The Old Woman, leaning in, added, "So, we're off to see Dr. Glaukomflecken again? I do hope he's ready for another chapter in the ongoing epic of my eyes."

"Yes, Dr. Glaukomflecken and his trusty monocle await, but I have every confidence that he'll guide you through this next challenge with the same flair and expertise he's known for."

Cunegonde sighed. "Back to Dr. Glaukenflecken—feels like déjà vu. This time, I'll make sure to remind him that we're focusing on deflating the Old Woman's eye pressure, not inflating his ego."

Rising to bid them farewell, the doctor offered a parting piece of advice. "Patience, humor, and a bit of courage have carried you this far. Keep those close, and I'm certain you'll navigate this next phase with grace as well as tenacity."

After their latest visit with Dr Guttata, Cunegonde and the Old Woman sought counsel from Martin, who reflected on the dizzying journey of Cunegonde and the Old Woman. "Ah, the Glaukomflecken-Drusen-Guttata merry-go-round, owned and operated by the Don Issachar Private Equity." Martin mused, "It sounds like you've been part of a very exclusive club, one that perhaps spins more than it advances. It's time we consider stepping off this carousel and find a more grounded path."

Cunegonde agreed. "The current circuit seems to have us going in circles. What do you have in mind, Martin?"

Martin nodded slowly, his expression thoughtful. "First, we must seek a second opinion. It's crucial we step outside the network

Don Issachar has woven around us. There are other specialists, ones not tied to this particular circuit, who might offer a fresh perspective."

Cunegonde's eyes brightened with a spark of hope. "That sounds promising. Do you know of anyone?"

"I do," Martin replied. "There's Dr. Leibniz in Geneva, renowned for his innovative holistic approach to ocular diseases. He's not part of any large conglomerate and values patient care over profit."

The Old Woman cackled, "A journey to Geneva? As long as it's not another roundabout, I'm in."

"I will email him tomorrow."

Chapter 19

It is often said that the effect is the unintended consequence of the cause. ~ Voltaire

With a sigh, Candide gazed out upon the utopian paradise of Eldorado. The sun glinted off the golden spires that dotted the landscape, birds sang sweet melodies in the trees, and a cool breeze brought the scent of flowers. Yet even in this perfection, Candide felt a gnawing emptiness.

"Ah, Eldorado," he mused. "A veritable Eden, overflowing with riches and delights the likes of which I've never known. But alas, my heart remains restless, for it is missing its other half, my dear Cunegonde."

At that moment, Cacambo came hiking up the garden path, back from another invigorating trek through Eldorado's countryside. "Candide, my friend!" he exclaimed. "What troubles you on this fine day in our paradise?"

Candide turned to his companion, a wistful look in his eyes. "Cacambo, do you not also feel a longing for the world beyond these utopian shores? As wondrous as Eldorado is, I confess its splendor now brings me only a little joy while separated from my love."

Cacambo's face fell at Candide's words. "It's true, I cannot deny I miss the thrills of our adventures abroad. But Eldorado has been a most gracious host! Are you certain you wish to leave this paradise?"

Just then, Pangloss came bustling up, his arms full of scrolls and tomes. "Come now, what's all this gloomy talk I overheard? Candide, the weather is perfect for a symposium on metaphysics and the nature of evil!"

Candide turned to his mentor, a sad smile on his face. "Dear Pangloss, ever the optimist. But I'm afraid even your philosophical discourses could not lift my spirits now. My mind is made up; I must be reunited with Cunegonde, even if it means leaving Eldorado behind."

Cacambo voiced his concerns, "But Candide, think of what we'll be leaving behind! The generosity of the Eldoradians, the bountiful feasts, the intellectual stimulation..."

Pangloss chimed in, "And the lively philosophical debates! Why, just yesterday I posited a new theory on the causes of evil in this world, though His Majesty argued quite persuasively . . . "

Candide stopped and turned to his friends, resolve in his voice. "My dear friends, I understand this paradise holds much to entice you. But without Cunegonde, it feels to me an empty splendor. Stay if you wish, but I cannot deny the longing in my heart."

After exchanging a look with Cacambo. Pangloss declared, "Well, an adventure with you is far better than the most lavish banquet alone! We shall accompany you, Candide."

Cacambo nodded. "Wherever the road may lead, we follow as friends."

Flanked by Pangloss and Cacambo, Candide entered the throne room. Before them sat the king. The king raised a hand in acknowledgement, inviting them to approach. Candide stepped forth, with Pangloss and Cacambo close behind. "Your Majesty," Candide began, "I come before you with a heavy heart, for I must request your permission to take leave of Eldorado."

The king's brow furrowed. "But why, my friend? Does not our kingdom provide all that you desire?"

"Indeed, it does, Your Majesty. But I long to find my lost love, Cunegonde. Without her by my side, even paradise feels lacking."

The king nodded slowly, empathy shining in his eyes. "I understand, Candide. The heart wants what it wants. You shall have my blessing to depart, though we shall miss your company greatly."

"You are most wise and generous, Your Majesty," Candide replied with a bow.

Pangloss stepped forward. "We appreciate your wisdom and generosity, Your Majesty. Our time here has been the pinnacle of enlightenment and fulfillment."

Cacambo gave a respectful bow. "Eldorado's splendor will forever live on in our memories, Sire. We thank you for your hospitality," he said with a warm and grateful smile.

"Before you depart, take provisions for your journey," the king offered. At his command, servants emerged bearing chests overflowing with gold, jewels, and supplies.

Candide's eyes misted with gratitude. "You honor us beyond measure, Your Majesty. We shall never forget your benevolence."

As they turned to take their leave, the king called out, "One last gift, my friends." Beckoning them over, he presented Candide with a box containing five regenfruits.

When they arrived at the royal stables, King Eldorado himself awaited them. Despite his sadness at their departure, he wished to see them off with the grace and generosity that defined his rule.

"My friends," spoke the king, "though you leave us, you will forever remain in our hearts. Please accept this gift as a token of our eternal gratitude." He motioned to the royal engineers, who unveiled the restored vintage jeep. Candide and his companions gasped in awe.

"Your Majesty, this is too generous!" Candide exclaimed. "We cannot thank you enough for your kindness and hospitality."

The king smiled. "It brings me joy to provide you with safe passage as you continue your journey. My engineers were fascinated by the opportunity to study such an antiquated combustion engine." The king of Eldorado approached the three companions, his expression solemn. "Remember, Candide, once you leave Eldorado, there is no returning. For you and your friends, the borders are sealed for eternity."

Candide bowed with deference before the king. "We understand, Your Majesty, and we are grateful for the time we've spent here. Your kingdom has shown us immeasurable generosity and wisdom."

Pangloss chimed in, "Indeed, we will treasure the philosophical discussions and debates we shared. The intellects of Eldorado are unparalleled."

Cacambo added, "And the vistas and landscapes were beyond comparison. Nowhere else have I witnessed such pristine natural beauty."

The king gave a warm smile at their words. "It brings me joy to know we have left positive impressions upon you. I have faith that you will find happiness and fulfillment in your travels beyond our realm."

Candide met the king's eyes. "We will never forget the kindness and hospitality you have shown us, Your Majesty. You gave us shelter and cared for us when we had nothing. We wish you and the people of Eldorado prosperity and peace."

With final farewells, the three companions took their leave, minds swirling with memories of their time in this mythical kingdom. As the jeep rumbled down the golden road leading out of Eldorado, Candide felt a pang of sadness. Yet his desire to reunite with his beloved Cunegonde was stronger than ever. Their journey was far from over, and somewhere out in the vast world, his love still waited.

Candide's mind wandered to the parting gift bestowed upon him by the benevolent king. He carefully opened the ornate box and examined its contents—five iridescent fruits glowing with an ethereal light.

"Pangloss, Cacambo! Behold these remarkable regenfruits gifted to us by His Majesty," Candide declared. "He said they possess the power to heal wounds, cure illness, even prolong life."

Pangloss's eyes widened with delight. "Astounding! I should very much like to study one. The scientific applications could be tremendous."

Cacambo gave a contemplative nod. "A king's gift is not to be taken lightly. We must use them wisely, my friends."

"Indeed," Candide agreed. "I shall save them for when they are truly needed." With that, he carefully tucked the precious box of regenfruits back into his satchel as the jeep continued its bumpy journey. His thoughts drifted to Cunegonde, picturing her radiant smile, imagining the joy of their reunion.

"Cunegonde's arms shall embrace me once more," Candide remarked with longing. "Her kisses will be sweeter than the ripest fruit."

Cacambo chuckled. "You wax poetic, my friend. But does your Cunegonde return the passion you feel?"

"I have no doubt!" Candide declared. "We were born for each other. Not even Eldorado could keep us apart."

"Let us hope the roads ahead lead swiftly back to her," Pangloss mused.

"I don't think we should return to the Jesuit hospital," Cacambo cautioned, his voice tinged with suspicion. "I have a feeling the administrator's sending us to the Oreillon village was not entirely holy in intent. We could head to Buenos Aires. I have a cousin there, who could help us."

"We also owe it to the king of Eldorado to keep his realm a secret, lest the Jesuits discover its existence," Candide added, his expression thoughtful.

Pangloss, who had been listening intently, spoke up. "You are right, Candide. We must tread carefully and honor the trust the Eldoradians have placed in us. Their secrets must remain safe."

Candide turned to Cacambo, his most trusted friend. "Cacambo, I have an important task for you. When we reach Buenos Aires, you must journey on to Miami. Seek out Cunegonde, the Old Woman, and Martin. Bring them to meet us in Bali."

"I will not fail you, Candide. Consider it done," Cacambo added, his determination evident.

Pangloss chimed in from the backseat. "While Cacambo gathers our friends, you and I shall sail onward to Senegal. From there we'll continue through Sri Lanka and Mumbai until we reach Bali."

Candide handed Cacambo a portion of the gold and jewels bestowed by the king. "Take these," he said. "They should provide enough for your travels and to care for the others."

The drive was long, but spirits were high, each lost in thoughts of adventures to come. At Buenos Aires airport, Cacambo, ever the practical one, gave each of them a warm embrace, his eyes betraying a hint of emotion. "Take care, my friends. We shall meet again," he said with a resolute smile. Candide and Pangloss returned the hug, their expressions a mix of sadness and hope.

Soon they, too, were aboard a ship, the ocean breeze rippling their hair. As the coastline of Senegal emerged on the horizon, a renewed sense of optimism and determination filled Candide's heart. He closed his eyes, picturing his reunion with Cunegonde. Though oceans still separated them, soon they would be in each other's arms. He would have the patience to wait a little longer.

Candide and Pangloss disembarked in Dakar, eager to explore Senegal's exotic landscapes and cultures. As they drove through the countryside, a small village came into view. Thatched huts dotted the dusty landscape, chickens and goats wandering freely. Children played in the dirt while women cooked over open fires.

As they approached a simple hut, Pangloss' eyes widened at the sight of the struggling family. The mother's slender frame looked weary as she tended the dusty crops, while her brood of children sat nearby, their sunken eyes and distended bellies, evidence of their hunger.

"Good woman, we couldn't help but notice your tribulations," Pangloss inquired with concern. "Please, allow us to be of what little assistance we can offer."

The mother regarded them with wariness at first, but desperation soon overcame distrust. "Bless you sirs, any help would be a godsend. My husband was injured in the mines, and I alone cannot provide for our children."

Just then, a cry rang out from within the hut. The mother's face creased with worry as she rushed inside. Candide and Pangloss followed close behind.

On a ragged cot lay a man, his leg crudely bandaged and stained with blood. His face was pale and damp with sweat. He was feverish and clearly in agony.

"My husband," the mother cried. "His leg was crushed in a mining accident. Without proper care, the wound has become infected."

Pangloss carefully examined the man's leg, shaking his head gravely. "This is beyond my skill to heal. But perhaps . . . " He looked at Candide.

With a nod, Candide reached into his pack and produced one of the precious regenfruits given to him by the king of Eldorado. "Here," he said, placing it in the man's feeble hand. "Eat this and be healed."

The man consumed the fruit weakly, but before long, color returned to his cheeks. He sat up, gazing in wonder as his fever subsided and the swelling and discoloration rapidly faded away. Standing, he tested his newly healed leg in amazement. The mother wept with joy.

"You have saved his life," she said. "However, can we repay you?"

"Seeing your family restored is payment enough," Candide replied. "May your days ahead be brighter," he said with sincerity, as he placed a diamond in her hand.

Candide and Pangloss arrived at the Blaise Diagne International Airport, eager to depart for their next destination. As they stood in line for their flight, Candide's mind drifted back to Cunegonde.

"We are but a few steps closer," Pangloss remarked, noticing the faraway look in Candide's eyes. "Each day, each mile we traverse, is one less between you and your heart's desire."

Candide nodded, clutching his bag a little tighter, feeling the weight of the remaining regenfruits inside. As the plane ascended, he gazed out at the African landscape receding below, its vast savannas and winding rivers slowly giving way to the endless horizon. He took a deep breath, readying himself for the journey ahead. Sri Lanka awaited

During their few days in Sri Lanka, Candide and Pangloss explored the exotic temples. One day, a scene caught their attention. An elderly woman, surrounded by her seven grown children, was offering prayers to the Hindu god Dhanvantari. Despite the woman's obvious signs of advanced dementia, her children cared for her with unwavering devotion. Their gentle touches and patient tones revealed the depth of their love, even in the face of such hardship.

Candide turned to Pangloss, clearly moved. "Look at the care and dedication those children show their mother. It's remarkable."

Pangloss nodded in agreement. "Yes, their filial piety is quite admirable." As they drew nearer, Candide was struck by the elderly woman's peaceful demeanor. Though her mind was fading, the comfort of her family kept her spirit content. Candide approached respectfully. "Good day to you all. I am Candide, and I couldn't help but notice your mother's condition. Is there any way I can assist your family?"

The eldest son gave them a gracious bow. "You are most kind to offer, good sir. Our dear mother's state fills our hearts with sorrow, yet caring for her together has brought us great joy."

Candide's compassion swelled. "Your devotion is truly noble. Please take this rare fruit. It may help restore your mother's health." Candide instructed them to give the regenfruit to their mother at dinner. He and Pangloss would return in the morning to check on her progress.

With hopeful hearts, Candide and Pangloss left the family to make preparations for the meal that could change their lives. The next morning, the two returned eagerly to the temple to check on the family. As they approached, a young woman ran up to them, her face etched with grief, tear trickling down her cheeks.

"Oh sirs!" she cried. "Your gift has brought both miracle and misery!"

Candide grasped her hands with concern. "What has happened, my dear? Please tell us."

The woman explained through tears, "The fruit cured my mother's mind, restoring her memories completely. But her temper and bitterness have also returned, driving us apart again."

Pangloss shook his head, incredulous. "It seems the cure has wrought unforeseen consequences."

"We had such joy caring for her gentle spirit," the daughter continued. "Now her moods and scolding have reopened old wounds between us siblings."

Candide's heart ached for their ordeal. "Is there anything we can do to help mend your family's bonds once again?"

The woman wiped her eyes, regaining some composure. "You have done enough, kind sirs. This is for us siblings to resolve, though the road ahead will be difficult. We thank you for your compassion."

With heavy hearts, Candide and Pangloss left the family to navigate their new challenges. The next day, Candide and Pangloss boarded a luxury cruise liner to Mumbai.

Chapter 20

*When it is a question of money, everybody is of the
same religion. ~ Voltaire*

After spending a week aboard the Opulent Mirage, a luxurious
five-star cruise liner, Candide and Pangloss disembarked in Mumbai. As Candide stepped out of the air-conditioned terminal and
into the sweltering Mumbai heat, sweat immediately beaded on his
forehead, reminding him of his arrival in Miami.

"Oh dear, it's hot enough to fry an egg on the pavement,"
Pangloss said, fanning himself with his Panama hat.

Candide replied with a wistful smile, "But what is this heat
compared to the fire that burns for Cunegonde in my heart? The
sun of Mumbai is but a candle next to it."

As a taxi rattled up, Pangloss prattled on, "This will be an
educational experience, my boy! A chance to experience the vibrant culture of India. Why, I daresay we shall be enlightened and
entertained at every turn."

Candide sighed. "Yes, enlightenment awaits us, as it always does. Yet, part of me longs not for new sights, but for a glimpse of my dear Cunegonde."

Pangloss sputtered more optimism, but Candide ignored him and climbed into the taxi, grateful for the full blast of the air conditioning. As the taxi sped into the chaotic streets, horns blaring, Pangloss nattered on about the architectural marvels and cultural landmarks they simply must see. Candide tuned him out, gazing out the window at the colorful shops and bustling crowds. His stomach rumbled, reminding him they hadn't eaten since breakfast. *How far is the hotel?* All he wanted was an ice-cold bottle of water, a turkey sandwich with white bread and mayo, a soft bed, and blissful silence. There were two more days before their flight to Bali, the final jaunt of this long journey. He hoped all was going as planned with Cacambo.

#

The next day, Candide and Pangloss were walking in front of a large country estate. Sitting in front of the gates, a young girl was crying. She was well dressed and well groomed, but tears streamed down her delicate cheeks.

Candide crouched beside her, offering a handkerchief. "There now, what's the matter?"

The girl sniffled, dabbing her eyes. "It's my father. He's dying."

"I'm so sorry to hear that." Candide glanced at the grand mansion looming behind wrought-iron gates. "Is your father inside?"

She nodded. "He has cancer. The doctors say he only has a few days left." Fresh sobs wracked her small body.

Candide asked in a gentle tone, "What's your name? How old are you?"

"My name is Aaradhya Patel, but you can call me Ari. I'm six years old."

Pangloss bent down and patted her shoulder. "There, there, child. No need to cry. I'm sure your father is receiving the very best medical care."

The girl shook her head, clutching Candide's handkerchief. "My brothers and sisters don't care. They're only concerned with inheriting his fortune. I'm afraid they won't even visit before he . . ." She trailed off, dissolving into tears once more.

Candide's heart ached for her. He helped her stand. "Come now, chin up. My friend Pangloss and I are doctors. Let's see what we can do to help."

The girl led them through a side door into the grand mansion, up a winding staircase, and down a long hallway to an ornate mahogany door. She pushed it open to reveal a spacious bedroom, elegant yet somber.

In the middle sat an enormous canopy bed, its burgundy curtains drawn back. A man lay still as death amidst the silken sheets, his skeletal frame barely making an imprint. His papery skin was tinged yellow, lips cracked and dry. IV tubes snaked under the covers while a nasal cannula delivered oxygen in futile bursts.

As Candide and Pangloss stepped closer to examine the man, a woman emerged from an adjoining washroom carrying a tray of medical supplies. "Professor Pangloss?!" she gasped, almost dropping the tray. "Is that *you*?"

Pangloss was nearly floored. He could not have imagined running into the woman who gave him syphilis and cost his job at the World's Best Medical School. His gaze slid over to Paquette, taking in her familiar heart-shaped face and ample figure. She was as ravishing as ever, though there were threads of silver in her chestnut hair that hadn't been there before.

Clearing his throat, Pangloss said, "Well, this is . . . unexpected."

Paquette's lips twisted into a wry smile. "Likewise, Professor. I never imagined we'd meet again after your dismissal from the university." Her gaze briefly scanned his threadbare coat and well-worn boots. "It seems the years have not been kind to both of us," she remarked with a touch of nostalgia, her eyes momentarily pausing on his prosthetic eye.

"No," Pangloss admitted ruefully. "Not as kind as one might have hoped. But we go on, as they say. The sun will rise again tomorrow."

Paquette's smile faded into a more somber expression. "That we do," she said softly. "Life marches on, ready or not."

Candide, who had been watching the exchange in silence, spoke up, "You know each other, then?"

"We were acquainted once, a long time ago," Pangloss said wistfully. "But that is a tale for another time." He shook off the lingering ghosts of memory and turned his attention back to Paquette. "Tell us, how did you come to be in the service of this household?"

Paquette waved a hand, dismissive. "The usual sad tale. Bad choices, worse luck, and too many indiscretions. Mr. Patel here took me in when I had nowhere else to go, and I've served as head chambermaid for nearly a year now." She sighed. "He is a good man. Stern, but fair. I don't know what will become of this place or me now that he's gone."

"His children will inherit the estate?" Candide asked.

Paquette snorted. "Inherit, yes, but take responsibility for it? I doubt that very much." She shook her head. "The vultures have already begun circling, I fear. They'll strip the place bare and turn out all the old servants who've served faithfully for years."

Pangloss, stroking his chin, probed further. "You said the children rarely visit. How many are there, and what are they like?"

"Three sons and four daughters," Paquette said with a grim expression. "Greedy, selfish, and cruel, the lot of them, except Ari. Not an ounce of compassion or decency between them." She glared in the direction of the door. "Mark my words, they'll be at each other's throats before the body's even cold."

Candide gave a regenfruit to Paquette and instructed her to give it to the dying man this evening with dinner.

"This fruit has remarkable healing properties," he said. "Give it to your master with his evening meal, and I believe you will see a great improvement in his condition."

Paquette took the fruit with hesitation. "Are you certain, sir? Mr. Patel is terribly ill. I do not wish to give him false hope or do anything that might worsen his condition."

"I have seen this fruit work miracles," Candide assured her. "At the very least, it will ease his discomfort and grant him a peaceful night's rest. But there is a chance it may do even more."

Paquette glanced between Candide, Pangloss, and the regenfruit, then gave them a slow nod. "Very well. I will give it to him as you instructed."

"We will return tomorrow to check on his progress," Pangloss said with a warm smile. Paquette smiled back, clutching the fruit in her work-worn hand.

While Candide and Pangloss made their way back to the inn in town, Pangloss sighed as if happily dreaming, his thoughts returning once more to the charming Paquette. "What a woman," he said with a grin. "So devoted and caring. It's no wonder I was smitten with her all those years ago."

Candide raised an eyebrow. "You seem to have forgotten she gave you syphilis and ruined your career."

Pangloss waved a hand. "Minor details. The heart wants what it wants, as they say!" He clapped Candide on the back. "I've promised to take her with us when we leave here. She has no desire to remain in the service of those vultures, and I aim to give her a better life."

Candide shook his head in amusement at his friend's foolish optimism. The regenfruit may work miracles, but even it would be hard-pressed to cure Pangloss of his selective memory and misguided passions.

The next morning, Candide and Pangloss made their way back to the estate, eager to see the effects of the regenfruit. The little girl greeted them at the gates, her eyes shining with hope.

"He's awake!" she cried. "The doctor came this morning and said his fever has broken and he seems to be recovering. Mama Paquette has been at his side all night."

Candide and Pangloss exchanged glances, barely suppressing their grins. It seemed the regenfruit had worked its magic once again.

The girl led them upstairs to the master bedroom, but when they reached the door, they found it locked. Muffled noises came from within—grunts, moans, and giggles. They froze in place, eyes wide.

Pangloss gulped. "I fear the regenfruit may have, er, overworked its miracles." Heart pounding, Candide threw his shoulder against the door. The lock splintered and the door crashed open.

Inside, they found the girl's father, hale and hearty, vigorously making love to Paquette amid the rumpled sheets. At the sound of the door crashing open, the couple startled and turned to face the doorway. The six older siblings stood clustered behind Candide and Pangloss, mouths agape at the scene.

Pangloss and the little girl yelled together, "Paquette! Father! What are you doing?!"

The couple broke apart, sheepish grins spreading across their faces. Paquette ducked her head, a flush rising in her cheeks, while the girl's father simply chuckled.

"What does it look like we're doing?" He pulled Paquette closer, nuzzling into her neck. She let out a contented sigh, tilting her head to give him better access. "This wonderful woman has given me a new lease on life. The least I can do is make an honest woman out of her."

Pangloss sputtered. "But—but—"

"No buts!" The father turned a stern eye on his six older children clustered in the doorway. "You vultures have been circling for days, waiting to pick over my corpse. You don't deserve a single rupee of my fortune. I'm leaving everything to my darling Paquette here, and my dear Ari. They're the only ones who genuinely care."

His children erupted into cries of outrage, but he silenced them with a glare. "Now get out! I have a wedding to plan, and a honeymoon to enjoy. Begone!"

They fled without another word. The father settled back against the pillows, pulling Paquette down to join him. "Now. Where were we?"

Candide took Pangloss by the arm, gently guiding him out of the room. "I think we've caused enough mischief for one day. Let's leave them to it." Stunned into silence, Pangloss didn't protest. As Candide quietly closed the door behind them, muffled laughter and the rustle of sheets drifted through the splintered wood. Retreating down the corridor, Candide and Pangloss exchanged wide-eyed glances, unsure whether to be amused or scandalized by this turn of events.

The image of Paquette's blissful expression burned into their minds. As they made their way back downstairs, Pangloss sighed. "Well. It seems Paquette has found her happy ending after all."

Candide shook his head in disbelief. "The regenfruit's powers know no bounds. For better and for worse, it seems."

Pangloss nodded, his hand absentmindedly scratching his head. "Such is the way of the world, my friend. Such is the way of the world."

#

The next morning dawned bright and clear. Candide awoke in their luxury hotel room to find Pangloss already up and dressed, anxiously pacing by the window.

"What is it?" Candide sat up, rubbing the sleep from his eyes.

"The police," Pangloss said with a grim expression. "They're waiting outside in the front of the hotel."

Candide blinked. "The police? Whatever for?"

"I suspect our escapades of yesterday have caught up with us." Pangloss pushed aside the curtain for a better look. "It appears the jilted siblings were not content to simply accept their disinheritance. I fear we're about to face the wrath of the legal system."

Candide groaned. "But we did nothing wrong!"

"The law can be a peculiar beast." Pangloss straightened his coat. "Best prepare yourself. I will do my best to defend you, but in a foreign land like this, there's no telling how things may unfold."

Resigned to reality, Candide got out of bed and dressed. By the time he emerged from the washroom, two officers of the law were knocking at their door.

Pangloss answered, adopting an air of casual innocence. "Good morning, officers. How may we help you today?"

The taller officer gave them a severe frown. "You both are under arrest for the unauthorized practice of medicine and distribution of unapproved drugs. Please come with us."

"This is preposterous! We are physicians!" Candide protested. But it was no use. They were promptly escorted from the hotel to face the local magistrate.

The magistrate was a stern-faced man with a thick mustache and pince-nez perched at the end of his bulbous nose. Wearing a peruke, he peered at them over the rims of his glasses, unamused. "You stand accused of a serious crime. How do you plead?"

Candide glanced at Pangloss, who gave an encouraging nod. He took a deep breath and said, "Not guilty, Your Honor. We acted with only the best of intentions."

The magistrate's eyebrows rose dubiously. "Acting with good intentions does not excuse breaking the law. You are not licensed to practice medicine in this country, yet you treated a patient and administered an unapproved substance. How do you justify this?"

Pangloss stepped forward, clearing his throat. "Your Honor, while it is true my young friend Candide does not hold a medical license in India, he is a graduate of the World's Best Medical School. He is more than qualified to treat any ailment. As for the treatment in question, it was not a medicine at all, simply a nutritious fruit, a gift of nourishment for the patient."

"Preposterous!" cried a voice from the gallery. Six well-dressed men and women strode forward, seething with fury. They were the siblings, who had pressed charges against the two men. The eldest brother spoke up, his face twisted in anger. "These charlatans nearly killed our father with their quackery! We demand justice."

The magistrate pounded the gavel to quiet them and peered down his nose at them. "You claim these men nearly killed your father, yet he seems quite healthy now. The fact that he has disinherited the lot of you is not a crime. On what grounds do you accuse them of wrongdoing?"

The siblings gaped at each other, momentarily stunned into silence. But they soon recovered, their voices rising into a clamor of protests. The magistrate banged his gavel, shouting for order.

Candide leaned close to Pangloss and whispered, "It seems they did not anticipate their father's recovery. Now their motives are laid bare, and justice may yet prevail!"

Pangloss smiled. "Have faith, my boy. The truth has a way of coming out, even in the unlikeliest of places."

The magistrate finally silenced the courtroom. "Enough! According to Indian law, any medical practice requires proper licensing and approval. It does not matter if the World's Best Medical School conferred twenty degrees upon you. Without sanction by the government, you have no authority to treat patients here."

Pangloss stroked his chin. "Your honor, while the law is quite clear on medical licensing, my client did not actually practice medicine. He merely offered the fruit as a gift. Its unexpected medicinal properties were incidental. And as no harm came to the patient, no wrongdoing occurred."

The siblings erupted into shouts of protest once more. The eldest brother cried, "They stole our inheritance through trickery and deceit!"

"Trickery?" Pangloss scoffed. "We restored your father to health. Ungrateful children like yourselves do not deserve such a gift. And we did not touch your inheritance!"

Candide, with a worried expression, tugged at Pangloss's sleeve. His companion's acerbic tongue would not win them any favors. But Pangloss smiled, unconcerned. He was filled with faith that justice would prevail.

The magistrate considered for a long moment. "While the defendants' actions were unorthodox, I find no evidence of adverse outcomes. However, under Indian law, you falsely claimed to be doctors before attending to the elder Mr. Patel. For that, justice must be served. I hereby sentence you both, Drs. Candide and Pangloss, if that is indeed who you are, to ten years in prison and a fine of 10 million rupees. Court adjourned!" He banged his gavel with finality.

The siblings let out a cry of cheer as the constables hand-cuffed Candide and Pangloss and ushered them away. The cheers faded into a dull echo as the heavy doors of the courtroom closed behind them.

In the dim light of the jail cell, Pangloss tried to uplift Candide's spirit. "My dear Candide, do not let this situation dampen your outlook on life. We have encountered worse predicaments and emerged unscathed."

Candide, however, was not so easily assuaged. "But ten years, Pangloss! And such an exorbitant fine! How ever shall we manage?"

Pangloss paced the small cell, his hands clasped behind his back as he pondered their dilemma. "I suspect we shall need to rely on our wits and perhaps a bit of fortune to extricate ourselves from this particular quandary. We must be patient."

Chapter 21

Life is thickly sown with thorns, and I know no other remedy than to pass lightly over them. The longer we dwell on our misfortunes, the greater is their power to harm us. ~ Voltaire

Candide shielded his eyes from the dazzling Bali sun as he disembarked from the plane. He breathed in the salty ocean air, a refreshing contrast to the stifling confines of the Indian prison. Cunegonde sprinted across the tarmac and leapt into his arms. Candide held her close, inhaling her familiar jasmine scent. After endless nights of despair in his cell, holding Cunegonde felt like coming home.

"My love, I thought I'd never see you again!" she cried, covering his face in kisses.

Cunegonde, the Old Woman, and Martin were preparing to leave for Geneva to visit Dr. Leibniz when Cacambo arrived in Miami. With Cacambo's assistance, they had been comfortably settled in Bali for several weeks. Upon hearing that Candide and Pangloss had been imprisoned in Mumbai, Cunegonde dispatched Cacambo and Martin to secure their release.

Over Cunegonde's shoulder, Candide spotted the Old Woman hobbling toward them. He winced at the gaping hole where her buttock once was.

"Don't look so glum, son," she cackled. "We're all back together now, eh? It'll take more than a little cosmetic damage to keep me down."

Candide smiled. "It's good to see you too, dear Old Woman."

Pangloss, Martin, and Cacambo approached, looking weary but triumphant.

"Quite an adventure getting you out of that prison," Martin said, clapping Candide on the back. "But nothing General Marshall, Cacambo, and I couldn't handle. Nice to have friends in high places."

"Yes, yes, very hush-hush black ops and whatnot. All I can say is that Martin is far more than a retired marine medic. Top secret stuff," Pangloss said, glowing. "The important thing is we're all here now, safe and sound."

Candide's joy dimmed. "Safe in this moment, perhaps, but far from sound. Our pockets are empty after paying the fine. All we have left are two measly regenfruits from Eldorado."

Cunegonde squeezed his hand reassuringly. "We'll get by. We always do."

Candide gazed at his ragged band of companions, amazed by their resilience. He may have lost his fortune, but he still had their love. For now, that would be enough.

As they made their way through the streets of Bali, the Old Woman led them to a small inn, its walls draped with flowering vines and its windows open to the sea breeze. "I may have lost a buttock," she said, "but not my knack for finding a decent place to rest."

That evening, they gathered around a worn wooden table outside the inn. Cunegonde served the two regenfruits. The fruit shimmered on the plate, emitting an ethereal glow.

Candide took a deep breath and turned to Martin and the Old Woman. "My friends, Cunegonde and I have discussed this at length. We want you to have the last two regenfruits."

Martin's eyes widened. "But Candide, those fruits could restore your health, your lost fortunes . . . "

Candide silenced him with a hand. "You both sacrificed so much for me and Cunegonde. Please, let me repay you in this small way."

The Old Woman cackled with delight. "Well, don't mind if I do!" She snatched one of the fruits from Candide's hand and devoured it.

Martin shook his head in amusement as he accepted the other fruit. "I won't argue with you, friend. Thank you." He took a bite and sighed with satisfaction.

Before their eyes, the companions witnessed an amazing transformation. The gaping hole in the Old Woman's backside filled in with new, supple flesh. Her clouded eyes cleared, regaining their sight. She looked decades younger, her skin glowing, her white hair, raven black once more.

"Look at me!" she cried, twirling. "I could almost forget the fifty years of my misfortunes!"

Martin's prosthetic legs fell away as strong, muscular new limbs grew in their place. He wiggled his new toes in wonder. Martin, with two new legs, did a mean moonwalk that would have made Michael Jackson envious!

"It's a miracle!" he remarked, a smirk betraying his usual gloom.

Candide grinned. "The least we could do for you both."

Over the next few months, the companions settled into a simple routine in their beachside village. Long days were spent fishing, gathering fruit, and enjoying each other's company.

One afternoon, Candide noticed a peasant working in the rice terraces below their hut. The man sang in a gentle cadence as he tended the shoots, his skin weathered from the sun and hands as rugged as the land he tilled. His face radiated profound contentment. His wife and seven children worked alongside him, their laughter floating in the breeze. They had so little, yet seemed so happy and fulfilled.

Intrigued by the peasant's apparent euphoria, Candide approached him, clearing his throat politely, he asked, "Good sir, might I inquire as to the source of your remarkable happiness? In my travels, I've encountered philosophers, kings, and scholars, yet none seemed as content as you, laboring here in your fields."

The peasant, pausing his work to wipe the sweat from his brow, looked Candide over with a mix of amusement and curiosity. "Happiness? In these fields? Friend, I think the sun has addled your brain. I'm just planting rice, not searching for the meaning of life."

"But surely," Candide pressed, "there must be something extraordinary in your life that grants you such peace. Have you discovered some great philosophical truth that eludes the rest of us?"

The peasant chuckled, a sound as grounded as the earth beneath their feet. "Philosophical truth? Look around you, sir. I have a family that loves me, a roof that doesn't leak too much, and enough rice to keep our bellies full. What need have I for philosophy when the mud between my toes speaks clearer than any scholar?"

Candide, taken aback, ventured, "But what of the world beyond these fields? The wars, the injustices, the endless quest for wealth and power? Do they not diminish your joy?"

The peasant, amused by Candide's earnestness, replied, "Ah, you speak of the world as if it were a beast that could be tamed by worrying. Tell me, does fretting over a storm cloud stop the rain? I choose to focus on my field, my family, and my flock. Let the kings and generals sort out the rest. As long as the rain comes and the sun rises, I have all I need."

The peasant resumed his work with a shrug. "Remember, friend, happiness grows where you water it. Now, if you'll excuse me, these rice paddies won't plant themselves."

Candide, with a newfound spring in his step, began to walk away, but paused and turned back momentarily. "One more question, if you'd indulge me, kind sir," he shouted, his voice carrying over the fields.

The peasant, bemused by Candide's relentless curiosity, paused his work once again, leaning on his hoe. "Go ahead, my friend," he replied, a smile playing on his lips.

"How do you deal with the unexpected? The calamities that life invariably throws your way?" Candide inquired.

The peasant laughed, a hearty sound that echoed across the surrounding fields. "Unexpected calamities? You mean like when the ox decides to play dead in the middle of plowing, or when the monsoon turns my field into a swimming pool for ducks?"

Candide nodded eagerly; his mind was ready to absorb more of the peasant's pragmatic wisdom.

"My dear fellow," the peasant began, wiping a hand across his brow, "life is much like this rice field. Sometimes, it's sunny and planting is easy. Other times, the heavens open up and you're knee-deep in mud. The trick isn't trying to control the weather—it's learning to dance in the rain and enjoy the muddy water squishing between your toes."

"And when the harvest is poor?" Candide probed further.

"When the harvest is poor," the peasant continued, "you share what little you have, you tighten your belt, and you plant again. There's always next season. Despairing over a bad crop only wastes time that could be spent preparing for the next."

Candide, moved by the peasant's resilience and simplicity, remarked, "You, sir, have given me more to ponder than all the lectures of Professor Pangloss. Your wisdom is the kind that truly cultivates the garden of the soul."

The peasant, finding the whole exchange rather amusing and slightly perplexing, shrugged. "Glad to be of service, though I suspect my *wisdom* is just common sense sprinkled with a bit of dirt. Now, if you'll excuse me, I have a real garden to tend to."

As he walked away, Candide furrowed his brow, pondering the significance of what he witnessed. After a lifetime of trials and tribulations, could this be the answer he long sought? If happiness existed, it was not found in wealth or status, but in embracing life's simple gifts. Friends, family, purpose—life's true meaning dawned on him there in that terraced field. With this epiphany blossoming in his heart, Candide's steps grew lighter as he made his way back to his hut, where Cunegonde was preparing dinner.

After dinner, Candide and Cunegonde settled onto the humble porch of their hut. Together, they watched the sunset give way to the stars, which emerged one by one, sparkling like diamonds strewn across the dark velvet of the night sky.

Candide turned to Cunegonde, who gazed out at the sparkling ocean. He took her hands in his.

"My love, I have traveled the world seeking happiness, never realizing it was here all along. After all we've endured, let us embrace this moment together."

Cunegonde met his eyes with a smile. "I wish nothing more than to share a life with you, simple as it may be."

Martin and the Old Woman approached, arm in arm. "What say, you two lovebirds? Shall we make it official?" Martin asked with a wink.

Candide laughed. "Indeed! Old friend, will you do us the honor of presiding over our union?"

"It would be my pleasure as long as you preside over ours." Martin replied, eyeing fondly at the Old Woman.

"I have a better idea," Candide exclaimed, his index finger shooting up in a burst of inspiration, before he dashed off.

Pangloss was summoned and preparations were made for an impromptu double ceremony on the beach at sunset. As the last rays of light faded over the horizon, the two couples exchanged vows of love and lifelong commitment as the wise professor led the double ceremony.

"Under the eyes of metaphysical and moral necessities, we gather to bind these souls in matrimony, proving that all is for the best, in this best of all possible worlds!"

They celebrated long into the night, dancing and feasting under the stars. Candide's heart swelled with joy. His journey had come to an end, but his new life was just beginning. Through struggles and misfortunes, he had finally found peace and purpose. There were no more grand questions to be answered or destinations to seek. For now, he had all he needed—his dear Cunegonde and their little patch of earth to tend.

The next morning, Candide was stirred from sleep by a knock at the door. He opened it to find a messenger bearing a letter.

"Pardon the intrusion sir, but I come with urgent news. Your benefactor, Mr. Thunder-ten-tronckh, has passed away. In his will, he left instructions that you should receive this upon his death."

Candide took the letter with shaking hands. He slit it open and read the contents with widening eyes.

"What is it, my love?" Cunegonde asked, roused from bed by the commotion.

"My benefactor . . . he has left me a vast inheritance," Candide replied in astonishment. "A parcel of land here on Bali overlooking the sea, plus a sizable trust for us to build a home and start a new life!"

Cunegonde gasped. "But how?"

"The letter says he was a longtime friend of my parents and watched me grow from afar. He wished to see me happy and secure." Candide beamed, embracing his new bride.

Soon Martin, Pangloss, the Old Woman, and Cacambo were gathered to hear the incredible news.

"With this gift, we can create a sanctuary for ourselves and help the less fortunate too," Candide declared. "Let's build an eye clinic for the poor and a place where we all can live in peace."

Everyone nodded in eager agreement, tears of joy in their eyes. After so much misfortune, it seemed providence had finally rewarded their faith.

#

In the evenings, as the sun set, casting a golden glow over their utopian dream, they would gather to reflect on the day's work. Pangloss would often remark, "See, despite our trials, we have found our purpose, proving my theory correct once again: that all is for the best, in the best of all possible worlds." To which Martin would retort, "Or perhaps it proves that even in a world rife with absurdity, we can carve out a slice of happiness."

Candide, looking out over the land that was now theirs, with friends and family by his side, would smile and say, "Let us continue to cultivate our garden, for it is in this simple act that we find true happiness."

Cacambo, ever practical, would remind them, "When philosophy fails, turnips won't."